KILLER KNIGHT

The long, grueling fight went on until Blade saw shadows creeping across the courtyard. As the sun began to set, it became harder and harder for Blade to see his deadly opponent. Blade had gambled on a quick and easy victory. The crowd was almost silent now. Blade wasn't sure how much longer he could stand. His shield arm seemed to be weighted with lead, and his shield was almost useless. The leather covering hung in strips where it wasn't ripped off completely, exposing bare wood. When his shield broke the battle would be over. Orric's vicious axe would see to that . . .

THE BLADE SERIES:

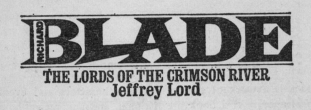

RICHARD BLADE

THE LORDS OF THE CRIMSON RIVER
Jeffrey Lord

PINNACLE BOOKS   NEW YORK

BLADE #35: LORDS OF THE CRIMSON RIVER

Copyright © 1981 by Book Creations, Inc.

An original Pinnacle Books edition, published for the first time anywhere.

Produced by Book Creations, Inc.
Executive Producer: Lyle Kenyon Engel

First printing, November 1981

ISBN: 0-523-41209-6

Printed in the United States of America

PINNACLE BOOKS, INC.
1430 Broadway
New York, New York 10018

THE LORDS
OF THE
CRIMSON RIVER

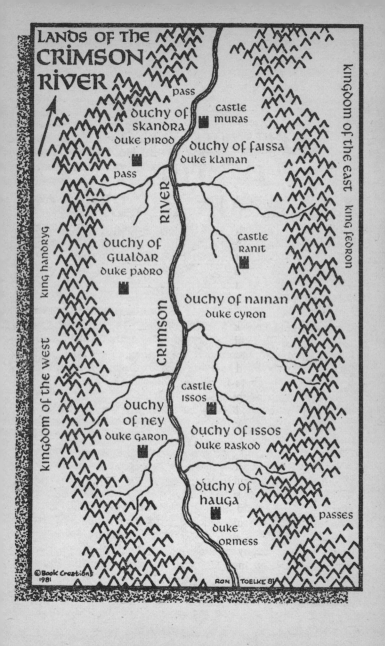

Chapter 1

"Bring it straight back when it's run," Lord Leighton told the programmer.

"There's a backlog," said the young man with the long but well-kept hair. "If you'd like me to give this priority—"

Leighton's desire to have the data back right away fought with his equally strong desire not to call unnecessary attention to what he was doing. The first desire won. "Give it priority, then. How long will it be?"

The man looked at his watch. "With luck, I should have it back by four o'clock. Without luck—" He shrugged.

Leighton smiled thinly. He knew everything that could happen to a computer much better than this young man ever would if he lived to be a hundred. Leighton had been working on computers before the programmer was born.

The programmer picked up the briefcase with the "*secret*" label on it and hurried out. Leighton sighed with relief, then leaned back in his custom recliner as far as his hunchback would let him. After a moment he closed his eyes and listened to the spattering of rain on the office window. He hoped a few minutes relaxing would get rid of his headache, but doubted it. Nothing would do that except learning if his latest scheme for Project Dimension X was all he hoped it would be. The next best thing would be to have the KALI capsule which sent Richard Blade into Dimension X back in operation. If he didn't get either of these, he'd be happy enough to get the Project's master computer back on line. He wasn't wildly optimistic about any of them.

The trouble started with Richard Blade's return from the

1

Dimension which held the city of Kaldak. He returned seated in a complicated piece of electrical equipment: one of the control chairs used for the fighting robots of the Dimension. Somehow, current had surged into the KALI capsule, but circuit breakers failed to operate, and Blade was brought back to Home Dimension in the chair instead. There was no damage to the computer, but with the KALI capsule heavily damaged and Blade's jaw broken when the chair fell over, the Project was going nowhere fast. While both the capsule and Blade's jaw were being fixed, it seemed like a good time to downline the master computer for a major inspection and overhaul.

Things could have been worse, of course. A year ago Leighton would have had to leave all the problems he couldn't tackle on his desk calculator to pile up until the main machine was back on line. That was when the whole top-secret Project Dimension X was concentrated in the complex two hundred feet below the Tower of London. Now things were different, although Leighton wasn't sure they were better.

As the Project grew, the complex got more crowded. The obvious solution was to move some of the Project's work aboveground.

Leighton himself thought this was a good idea. So did J, the quiet gray-haired spymaster in charge of the Project's security. So did Richard Blade, in many ways the most important man of the three. Years after one of Leighton's computer experiments led to the discovery of travel into alternate Dimensions, Richard Blade was still the only living man who could make these dangerous journeys and return alive and healthy.

When Leighton, J, and Richard Blade all agreed on doing something for Project Dimension X, it was as good as done. It took only a few days to find a building for sale in a suburb of London, and only a few weeks to move a good part of the Project into it. They were careful to move only those parts of the Project which wouldn't give away much of the Dimension X secret, although security precautions were as rigid as ever.

Complex Two still needed a great deal of computer capacity. The master computer could not have any terminals outside the underground Complex One without compromising its security. So the new building needed hardware of its own. After a few hundred thousand more pounds were pried loose from the secret funds, Complex Two got its own computer. If Lord Leighton was willing to commute back and forth between the complexes, he could now play with computers twenty-four hours a day.

For a while Leighton nearly did this. His eighty-odd years, his hunchback, and his polio-twisted legs didn't slow him down very much. They didn't slow down his mind at all. It was as quick and fertile as ever, devouring facts and jumping ahead to bold conclusions the same way it had for nearly sixty years. It worked that way when Leighton sat down to consider the problem of Blade's return from Dimension X.

Every time Blade went into Dimension X, he was wired into the master computer so that its electronic mind and his human one were linked. Leighton always took great care to make that link as complete and predictable as possible, and the KALI capsule, which encased Blade's body so that almost every inch of his skin was in contact with wire electrodes, had been a great success. But some of Leighton's experiments along those lines had been less than successful. He still shuddered at the memory of the automated KALI computer, which had unleashed the Ngaa monster on the world. Blade had nearly been killed, more than thirty other people had died, and both the Project and the whole world had been put in a deadly danger, from which Blade had to save them at the risk of his life.

Still, Blade's departure for Dimension X was now pretty much a matter of routine. His return from Dimension X, on the other hand, followed no pattern Leighton could discover. Somehow the computer reached out across space, time, and Dimension to link itself with Blade's mind and twist it back into its normal patterns, so that he once again saw and heard and moved through Home Dimension England. What was more, the computer almost always waited until Blade's work in Dimension X was completed. It seemed as if Blade and the computer *remained* linked in some way after Blade's departure.

It was even more maddening that the computer also

3

brought back whatever Blade was holding or even close to at the time. He'd seldom been able to take any equipment into Dimension with him. Several times this nearly cost him his life, and it ruled out any idea of really exploring Dimension X. Coming back, however, Blade had brought everything from jeweled knives to a full-grown live horse!

This was the kind of mystery Lord Leighton didn't like at all. It weakened his control over the most vital experiment he'd ever performed, an experiment vital to the future of the whole world as well as to his own career and reputation. Blade's discoveries in other Dimensions, as well as the things he brought back with him when he returned home, provided the knowledge and power to make England a great power once again, to make Leighton a great man, and to make the world better off than it had ever been. But the mysteries still attached to traveling in other Dimensions made Leighton look as if he didn't quite know what he was doing, and he would cheerfully have sold his soul to the Devil to avoid that fate.

Unfortunately the Devil wasn't buying. Lord Leighton had to puzzle things out as best he could, and his best wasn't good enough. There were other problems, too. The Project's budget was generous, but it wasn't infinite. Also, J always made a fuss over experiments and innovations which put Blade in unnecessary danger.

So Leighton was groping in the dark until Blade returned from Kaldak. Unlike the KALI capsule, the control chair that brought him back was nearly intact, ready for Leighton's examination. He tested it every way he knew of and a few more he invented on the spot. All the tests showed the same thing: the master computer not only generated a powerful electrical field matching Blade's brain waves, but projected it to wherever Blade was in Dimension X. The chair, with all its complicated equipment, had become part of that electrical field and had come back to Home Dimension with Blade seated in it.

It wasn't news that the computer generated such an electrical field. It was news that it could project it so far. Could it possibly project the same field, to *send* Blade? Did he have to be wired into the computer or at least encased

4

in the KALI capsule? Or did he only have to be within reach of the appropriate electrical field?

Leighton started working twelve and fourteen hours a day on this question. At last he reached the point where he needed to run all his work through a computer. By then the repairmen had the master computer down for its overhaul, and Leighton was left with the smaller computer in Complex Two.

That wasn't a problem in itself. The new computer had all the capacity Leighton needed. Unfortunately, in expanding its facilities the Project had also expanded its bureaucracy. There were established procedures for using the new computer, which Leighton himself could only ignore at the price of drawing a good deal of attention. This was the last thing he wanted, at least until after the first few runs. He always preferred to work out at least a preliminary proposal before talking to anyone else. The ultimate solution to that problem would be a personal computer of his own, but that wasn't practical yet.

An adequate computer would cost at least fifty thousand pounds. While Leighton held enough patents to be a fairly wealthy man, he wasn't yet in a position to sink that sort of money into something which would be no more than a convenience.

Leighton cracked his knuckles, stretched, and looked at the clock on the wall. The run was taking longer than the programmer promised. He picked up a notebook and pencil from the table and began doodling rough sketches of a possible electrical-field generator linked to the master computer. It looked rather like an oversized telephone booth, with Blade standing in the middle.

A new thought struck Leighton. Standing freely, Blade could wear anything which wouldn't disrupt the electrical field. He wouldn't need to keep his skin bare for the electrodes of the earliest system they'd used in the Project or for the conducting lining of the KALI capsule. He could go into Dimension X with clothes on his body and boots on his feet, carrying weapons, food, water, and survival gear. This would improve both Blade's chances of survival and his ability to explore Dimension X.

5

The new method might also reduce the strain on the subject's mind and body. If that happened, perhaps somebody else could *finally* go into Dimension X and come back alive and sane! That would be an even bigger breakthrough than equipping Blade. Right now the Project depended entirely on Blade, and sooner or later his luck might run out. Even if it didn't, he would someday be too old for such demanding work. If there wasn't somebody ready to take over by then, the whole Project would come to a halt. *That,* thought Leighton, *would be a damnably silly ending to my career!*

The notebook was nearly filled with sketches by the time the programmer returned with the completed runs and a pot of tea. Leighton noticed the man's eyes lingering on the notebook, quietly shut it, and poured himself a cup of tea. The young man looked embarrassed and slipped out in a hurry.

Leighton sipped the tea and chuckled. He really shouldn't have been so obviously suspicious. All the people in Complex Two had been investigated as thoroughly as those working underground. That programmer could be trusted. He swallowed some more tea and started flipping through the print-outs. His excitement grew with each page.

Chapter 2

Lord Leighton wouldn't have been so sure about the programmer's loyalty if he'd known the man was also an undercover agent for MI6A. He was supposed to watch for any signs of hostile espionage in Complex Two and also for any irregularities in the management of the Project itself.

Lord Leighton would have also been infuriated to learn

that J knew all about the programmer's undercover activities. J had agreed to have Leighton spied on only after a long argument with the Prime Minister. J knew that Leighton was loyal, as well as rich enough to be nearly unbribable. His private vices, if any, were really nobody else's business. He also knew what Lord Leighton would think of his being spied on.

The Prime Minister turned a deaf ear to everything J said. "I don't necessarily disagree with you," he said. "But Leighton isn't the whole Project. At least fifty other men could make off with a good deal of money or valuable supplies if they had a chance. We can't afford to leave them unwatched. Surely Leighton will understand that we're not after *him*?"

J shook his head. "He might, but it wouldn't make any difference. He only tolerates security against espionage. Otherwise, he'll defend any scientist against us as if we'd attacked him personally."

"If he's that thin-skinned, do you think he's really suitable as director of the Project?"

There was no point in wasting tact on anybody capable of such an idiotic remark. J shrugged. "I hardly think that matters. There's certainly no one else suitable."

The Prime Minister decided to reply as bluntly. "Very well, J. I'll put it as a direct order. Your people in the Project are to keep watch for *any* irregularities, not just foreign intelligence activities. I'll put that order in writing, so there won't be any question about what happens to you if it isn't carried out. Or would you rather retire now? We can keep this matter quiet if you do. You're gifted, J, but you're certainly not as unique as you say Leighton is."

The only really adequate reply to those words would have been to punch the Prime Minister in the nose. Since this was out of the question, there was really nothing J could do except go along and have Leighton's activities watched. The Prime Minister was partly right. Watching over the Project's security meant more than looking for Russian spies and English embezzlers. It meant looking out for Richard Blade and looking after Lord Leighton.

So J gave his undercover man in Complex Two the appropriate orders and hoped the young man would know

7

when to turn a blind eye. For a while it looked as if his hopes would be justified.

Then came the eager call describing Leighton's new studies of the computer's electrical field and what he might be planning to do with them. J listened politely until he could find an excuse for hanging up, then poured himself a whiskey so large that his doctor would have screamed in protest. He sat down with the whiskey in his hand, staring out at another dismally gray and rainy London afternoon.

He was going to have to act on this call, even if he thought the young man was jumping to conclusions. Leighton certainly seemed to have another bee in his bonnet. If the bee buzzed loudly enough, sooner or later the Prime Minister would hear it. Then there'd be questions asked, including why J hadn't informed the P.M. before.

Also, there was Richard Blade to think about. Leighton's brainstorms sometimes created new and unnecessary dangers for Richard. Even if the younger man hadn't been almost a son to J, the old spymaster would have had to protest at putting the Project's only reliable test subject in unnecessary danger.

The first thing to do, however, was call Richard himself. J drained the glass, went to the scrambled telephone in the corner, and began punching in Blade's number.

It took J quite awhile to reach Blade, because the younger man wasn't at home or even in London. He was in Hampshire, miles from the nearest telephone, looking at a country house he wanted to buy.

The real-estate agent fluttered around Blade like some annoying but harmless insect, humming the praises of the house. He seemed totally undaunted by the fact that the black-haired man beside him was nearly twice his size, six foot one and two hundred and fifty pounds, all of it muscle, which even Blade's heavy tweed sports jacket couldn't conceal. If Blade had wanted, he could have crushed the man like a fly.

Instead Richard Blade tried to ignore him. He already knew everything he needed to know about the place. It would be nearly perfect for him, and it would also cost much more than he could afford. The initial cost wouldn't

8

be outrageous for a house, outbuildings, and thirteen acres of land. It was making the place fit to live in that would break him. The house was built around 1760, and it had never really been modernized. Even worse, the last two owners hadn't bothered to keep the place up properly. Blade wasn't about to bankrupt himself doing all the work they'd left undone over the last fifty years.

The agent was still talking. Blade listened briefly, decided he still wasn't saying anything important, and started doing mental arithmetic. He wanted the house so badly he could taste it. He also wanted to find some flaw in his previous calculations which would let him make an offer. All his training and experience warned him against this sort of wishful thinking, but this time he wasn't facing a KGB agent or some monster in Dimension X. This was his private life, and he was damned well going to do some wishful thinking if he felt like it.

Unfortunately all Blade's desire for the house couldn't make the figures come out in his favor. He would still be a good fifteen thousand pounds short. He was about to cut off the agent's humming when a thought struck him. "Are you allowed to sell an option on this house?" he asked.

The agent looked at him for a moment as if "option" were a word in Chinese. Then an unmistakable look of eagerness passed over his thin face, and he nodded.

By the time they'd finished sketching out the terms for an option agreement, the rain was coming down in sheets. Blade hoped none of the low spots in the dirt lane back to the highway would flood. The idea of being marooned here all night with no better company than the real-estate agent was unappealing.

For three thousand pounds, half of it refundable, Blade could buy an exclusive option on the house for six months. That would give him time for the next trip into Dimension X, no matter how long it took to fix the KALI capsule. His broken jaw was completely healed, and he himself was fit and ready to go.

The option would also give him time to try bargaining with the real-estate firm on the price of the house. From the agent's eagerness over the option, his firm hadn't had a decent offer on the house for years. They might be willing to bargain, particularly if Blade didn't need a mortgage. He hoped they wouldn't ask too many questions about where his cash came from.

Apart from its condition, the location of the house made it suitable only for someone who wanted to be fairly close to London, but otherwise wanted as much solitude as he could get in southern England. That was a perfect description of Blade. He'd always been a man who preferred to walk alone, like a cat. Otherwise he'd never have gone into intelligence work and then into Project Dimension X. As time went by, his experiences in Dimension X set him more and more apart from everyone else in the world. He'd long since stopped caring about the London party circuit, with its light chatter, light minds, and light women who could give him a night's pleasure but not a minute's real companionship.

Then he came home from the forest of Binaark with the semi-intelligent hunting cat, Lorma. He wasn't going to let her spend the rest of her life in the hands of the Project's veterinarians, and their curiosity be damned! As soon as he was out of the hospital after his trip to Kaldak, he started looking for a country house. Now he'd found one, if he could only get the price down!

Blade climbed into the Rover and turned on the headlights and engine. Then he put the car in gear and started his slow creep back down the lane. Behind him the house was now completely invisible in the rain and the gathering twilight.

Blade didn't drive back to London that night. He checked into a hotel in Basingstoke, ate a good if overpriced dinner with plenty of whiskey and soda, then called his home for any recorded messages. As soon as he'd heard what J left, he called the number J used when Blade or a select handful of other people weren't using a scrambled phone.

As usual, nobody answered. Blade sipped at his drink, then said, "Record. J, this is Richard, returning your call. I'm at the Golden Keys in Basingstoke," and gave the hotel's telephone and his own room number. "I'll come straight to the branch office. I should be there by ten A.M.

10

"I certainly think we ought to discuss this matter with His Excellency [a code name for Lord Leighton]. But I think we should put it in the form of a question—does he have any new investment plans? That should also conceal the sources of our information. End recording."

Blade suspected that telling J to be tactful with Lord Leighton was like teaching his grandmother to suck eggs. But you couldn't be too careful in dealing with Lord Leighton, with his improbably brilliant mind and impossibly short temper. Also, J sometimes behaved toward Blade like a mother hen with one chick. Blade knew why J did this, and also knew it could sometimes cause more problems than the Project could tolerate.

Whatever J said to Leighton, Blade hoped he'd say it before Leighton discovered that his secret scheme wasn't a secret anymore. Otherwise there wouldn't be much chance of avoiding a bloody awful scene. Blade shuddered at the thought, considered having another drink, then decided against it. He was going to be getting up early if he wanted to be in London by ten tomorrow morning. He did a quick one hundred and fifty push-ups; then with his pajamas and towel over his arm, he walked into the bathroom.

Chapter 3

Unfortunately, Leighton worked faster and better than either J or Blade expected. He not only discovered that the cat was out of the bag but who'd let it out. When J learned everything the scientist had done to discover the secrets, he was impressed. He even told Leighton, "You might have had quite a career in intelligence work, if you'd wanted it."

By then Leighton and J were on speaking terms again,

11

so the scientist didn't tell J what he could do with intelligence work and intelligence agents. He merely grunted and raised his bushy white eyebrows higher than usual.

The morning Blade came to Complex Two, however, things were different. It wasn't at all certain that the two older men would ever be on speaking terms again. Blade suspected that Project Dimension X came closer to being wrecked that morning than it had since the affair of the KALI computer.

He walked into Leighton's office just before ten. The cordon of guards and secretaries outside were trying very hard to pretend there was nothing wrong. Blade knew that look and what it might mean, and sighed. He'd rather fight a tiger bare-handed than walk into what probably lay beyond that soundproof door, but there were no tigers around.

He opened the door to hear a tight, controlled "—accusation is not only ridiculous, it's adding insult to injury," from Leighton. Blade shut the door as J replied. His voice was not as controlled as Leighton's, and his face was the color of a ripe strawberry.

"Do you think you've been injured?"

"I *know* I've been injured," replied Leighton. "Spied on in my own office, at my own work, over matters which have nothing to do with Project security. What are you trying to do, find something you can use to blackmail me?"

J's face got even redder at that charge, but he fortunately couldn't find his voice. That gave Blade his chance. He'd have liked to wait until he knew a little more about what had really happened, but didn't think he had time. The two men needed a peacemaker right now.

"I think that's a rather wild accusation itself, if you don't mind my saying so," said Blade. He looked at Leighton in a way which clearly showed he didn't care if Leighton minded or not. This got Leighton's attention long enough for J to catch his breath and recover his voice.

"I agree," he said. "Blackmailing you never entered my mind. I admit that our man was overzealous—"

"Overzealous!" exploded Leighton. His eyebrows and hair were bristling as if they were charged with electricity.

12

"That damned young puppy has made it impossible for me to trust—"

"What is all the fuss about, sir?" asked Blade. He hoped this pretense of innocence would fool Leighton, and perhaps diffuse the volatile situation.

Leighton sighed. "I suppose I'd better go back and tell Richard exactly what's happened. I imagine you've already given him your version, J. Now it's my turn. With your permission?" he added sarcastically.

J nodded. "Be my guest."

Before long, Blade was so interested in Leighton's ideas about the computer's electrical field that he was forgetting to be angry over the scientist's bad manners to J. No doubt about it—Leighton had conceived a brilliant theory. If it worked out in practice, it might be the biggest breakthrough in the history of the Project.

Would it work out in practice, though? Or would it become another KALI computer? They couldn't be sure without a full-scale test, and J was apparently in no mood to permit that. He thought Leighton was trying to sneak a major change in the Project past him. Leighton thought J was trying to take over the scientific part of the Project.

There was enough right on both sides to make it hard for Blade to choose between them. If both men hadn't lost their tempers, they'd probably have already seen this for themselves. The damage was done, however. Now it was up to Blade to repair it.

For a moment he was tempted to tell Leighton about the Prime Minister's order to J. If the scientist knew J wasn't entirely his own master in this affair, he might calm down. Unfortunately, this wasn't Blade's secret to reveal. J wouldn't have even told Blade if they hadn't been so close for so long.

"How long before the KALI capsule is fixed?" Blade asked Leighton. "The last time I heard, it would be about another month."

The scientist's face twisted as if he'd bitten into a rotten fruit. "Now it's about six weeks. We've found a few more parts which need replacing. We've already cannibalized everything we can from the spare capsule. So now everything new has to be hand-built. . . ."

13

"I see." Blade looked at the sketches of the field-generator booth spread across Leighton's desk. "How long would it take to build and test one of these?"

Blade wished Leighton wouldn't grin so triumphantly. "About three weeks. The beauty of this is that we can use off-the-shelf components for most of it."

"Provided that they give an adequate margin of safety, yes," put in J.

Leighton's mood was so much improved that he ignored the remark and went on. "With this system we don't have to be nearly as precise outside the computer itself. The field strength can vary up to twenty-five percent and still be effective—and safe," he added, as J opened his mouth.

"Then it seems to me Lord Leighton ought to go ahead with the field-generator booth," said Blade. "He can have it ready in half the time it will take to repair the KALI capsule. It'll certainly be safer than using the KALI capsule in its present condition"—Leighton nodded—"and we can be careful this time around."

"Exactly what do you mean by that?" said J. He sounded as if he was now suspicious of Blade's motives instead of Lord Leighton's.

Blade held up one of the sketches. It showed a stick figure wearing a heavy pack and bristling with enough weapons for three men. "It will be safer because I'll be so well equipped, though in this one His Lordship has me loaded up like a pack mule. I suggest we start with something a little simpler. Say shorts, footgear, a canteen, and some sort of easily hidden weapon."

Leighton leaned back in his chair and made a steeple of his fingers. "That's a reasonable suggestion. We can use the same fabric we used for Richard's loincloths when we were using the capsule and the electrodes. It may not make the trip, but at least we know it isn't dangerous. If we can waterproof it, we can make a canteen. With extra layers, we can make sandals."

"What about the weapons?" asked J. Blade was relieved to hear J sound merely curious now, instead of suspicious of anybody.

"That depends on what you want, Richard. If you can

14

manage with a knife, we have more than enough Englor Alloy Two to make one."

The nonconducting alloy from Englor had also been thoroughly tested. A loinguard made of it had survived Blade's trip to Kaldak and back. He nodded. "A knife will be easier to make and definitely easier to hide. Also, it won't make anyone in a pretechnological Dimension suspicious the way a gun would." He thought for a moment, then added, "If you ever want to make a long-range weapon for me, try a crossbow instead of a gun."

"One thing at a time," said Leighton. "We've got the production of EA Two up to five pounds a week, but that's much less than what we'll need before long. We could triple it at once with enough money for—"

"If Richard survives this experiment, I'll support your request for more money," said J.

"If I survive it, I think we won't have much trouble getting the money," said Blade. "This is going to be a big step forward."

"Are you both quite through telling me things I already know?" said J testily. Blade and Leighton looked at each other, then nodded. "Very well. Go ahead, Leighton, and good luck to both you and Richard."

Blade caught up with J in the parking lot. The older man was standing with his bowler hat in one hand and his rolled-up umbrella in the other. He turned as he recognized Blade's step behind him.

"Ah, Richard. Thank you for playing peacemaker. I sometimes wonder if I'm getting too old for my job. Ten years ago I'd never have let someone like Leighton bait me into losing my temper."

"There isn't anybody like Leighton, when it comes to a sharp tongue," said Blade mildly. "Or if there is I never want to meet him. Besides, ten years ago we weren't involved in anything quite as important as the Project."

"No, we weren't," said J. "But I still shouldn't have lost my temper. And you shouldn't have agreed so enthusiastically to going along with Leighton's brainstorm. It's only going to encourage him to be careless—some other time, if not this one. Richard, I have to ask you. Do you think your judgment is slipping? I'd hardly blame you if it was, considering all that you've been through, but . . ." He let his voice trail off.

Blade nodded. He understood J's reason for the question. Apart from his personal affection for Blade, J was worried about his sense of self-preservation. The popular notion about secret agents being daredevils was a long way from the truth. They had to be brave, of course, and never hesitate to take necessary risks. They had to be equally firm against unnecessary ones, and good at telling the two apart. Field agents who didn't learn this were dangerous to themselves, their comrades, their informants, and the security of their organizations. Blade knew of cases where an agent's own people terminated him because he was too fond of unnecessary risks. Sometimes even an experienced agent like Blade started losing his grip, and if that was the case now, the sooner J knew the better.

Blade shrugged. "I'd probably be the last one to know if I was getting sloppy. Dimension X is a completely unpredictable environment, so it's hard to say what's an unnecessary risk. I don't really think I'm in trouble, though. Not yet. Besides, with Leighton's field-generator booth, my safety seems more certain than ever—not to mention the safety of some other Dimension X traveler, should such a candidate ever present himself." *Or herself,* Blade thought. Sooner or later, there would be *someone* else besides Blade. The only question was, *who?*

Lord Leighton was better than his word, not only about producing the field-generator booth quickly but also about testing it thoroughly. The list of tests he'd performed on its components ran to six typewritten pages. By the time the booth was ready, Leighton was a red-eyed, tottering wreck, who looked every day of his age. J practically ordered him to put off the trip for a couple of days in order to get a decent night's sleep and a few solid meals.

Blade spent the extra days finishing the paper work on the option for the country house and saying good-bye to Lorma. On past trips there'd always been a last night or two with girl friends. This time there wasn't any human being Blade felt as close to as he did to Lorma, except for J and Lord Leighton. He knew he shouldn't feel this much apart from his fellow human beings, but doubted he could do anything about it. His experiences in Dimension X were driving him further and further apart from the rest of the human race in this Dimension, and that was all there was to it.

In the familiar changing room carved out of the rock wall of the underground Complex One, Blade went through an unfamiliar routine. He started as usual by stripping himself naked and smearing himself with rancid-smelling grease for protection against electrical burns. He used a lighter coating than he'd ever used before, though, one barely visible against his tanned skin. Then he began pulling on the new equipment.

There was the wire loinguard. There were blue water-proof shorts over them, with a belt of the same material. On the belt he tied a collapsible fabric canteen with a rub-ber stopper and sandals built up from several layers of the fabric. Finally he picked up a stiff cloth sheath and tied it to his left arm. Inside the sheath was a knife made entirely of Englor Alloy Two, except for a thin coating of plastic on the handle to give a better grip. It was a duplicate of the famous Fairbairn-Sykes fighting knife used by the British Commandos in World War II. Forty years later it was still one of the best combat knives around, particularly in the hands of a trained fighter like Blade.

Blade looked at himself in the mirror, trying to get used to the new image. He decided it was going to take awhile. He looked like a cross between a champion weight lifter and a California surfer. He stepped out of the changing room and started threading his way through the consoles of the computer. He wasn't sure if he felt overdressed or un-derdressed, but he couldn't shake off the feeling that *some-thing* was wrong with the amount of clothing he had on.

At last he reached the spot in the center of the computer where the KALI capsule had stood. In its place was the amazingly simple field-generator booth, a rectangular frame of light steel I-beams completely encased in fine-gauge wire. The box stood freely on a thick insulating pad of rubber. The only thing which still bothered Blade slightly was the small size of the booth. There'd be only a few inches of air between him and the charged wires on all sides. Making the booth much larger would have meant heavy insulation all around, though, or the risk of affecting the computer. That would be far more dangerous to Blade than an electrical field, which Leighton could always cut off at the touch of a button.

That was the real beauty of the new system, as even J had to admit. Its success depended primarily on the computer, which was a tried and tested precision instrument, capable of being adjusted to the finest tolerances the human mind could imagine. Right now it was probably working even better than usual, thanks to its recent overhaul. It could generate a field matching Blade's brain waves with no trouble at all, and that was the only thing which had to be done exactly right. Everything else in the operation of the field-generator booth had a bigger margin for error built into it than Blade hoped they'd ever need.

He realized suddenly that Leighton and J were both staring at him. He'd been woolgathering while they were waiting for him to step into the booth and get their part of the job over with. He mentally kicked himself and took a deep breath.

"I'm ready."

Leighton pressed a button on a hastily rearranged master control panel, and the booth rose into the air. To make sure the electrical field was even all around Blade, the mesh was one unbroken piece. The only opening in the booth was at the bottom. For Blade to get inside, the booth was lifted off the rubber pad by a winch, then lowered back over him. As the booth settled back in place over Blade, he shifted his footing to give himself as much room on all sides as he could.

"Ready, Richard?" said J. Blade would have given a thumbs-up sign, but he didn't dare raise either arm that far. Instead he nodded.

Lord Leighton's hand came down on the master switch. The world around Blade turned into a blaze of light, forcing him to shut his eyes. For a moment all was silence, then he heard an ominous crackling and smelled pungent smoke. Had the experiment failed? Even worse, had it started an electrical fire in the complex?

Chapter 4

A moment later, the smells in the smoke told Blade he'd made the transition safely and was in Dimension X. He identified burning wood, straw, and manure, as well as another stench which a man never forgets once he's smelled it for the first time.

Burning human flesh.

Somewhere close at hand was battle, fire, or disaster.

Blade opened his eyes. He was standing in the same position he'd been in when Leighton pulled the switch, with all his equipment and clothing apparently intact. He was also facing a weathered timber wall with smoke oozing out of the joints between the boards. On top of the wall a thatched roof was blazing, dropping embers and hot ashes all around Blade. On either side was more smoke, a few dimly seen figures scurrying through it, and other figures lying still on the ground. Behind Blade was a stand of evergreen trees. He quickly retreated into their cover, then pulled on his sandals. If he'd had time, he would have savored this pleasure of putting something on his feet, but this looked like a good place to leave as soon as possible.

Blade started moving through the trees to his right, to get clear of the burning barn at least. As he moved, he started hearing the sounds of battle. When he reached a place opposite the village square, he saw that the village was the scene of a battle between two bands of medieval-looking armored knights. Both sides were mostly on foot, with only a few mounted men. One side wore black plumes on their helmets, while their opponents wore green gloves on their left hands.

19

Otherwise there wasn't much difference between the two bands. Both wore knee-length coats of mail with plate reinforcements on their lower legs, forearms, and chest. Their helmets were all open-faced. Either archery wasn't used, or they preferred clear vision to protection against an arrow in the face. From the way they moved and used their weapons, they were all trained and experienced fighters.

Blade was particularly well qualified to judge their fighting skill. He'd been a member of the Medieval Club during his days at Oxford, and worked out several times a week with replicas of medieval swords, maces, and shields. This skill had saved his life in several Dimensions. It now looked as if this might be another one where such skill would be useful.

Most of the villagers seemed to have already left, either fleeing or, perhaps, being carried off by the knights. Blade decided to follow them. He couldn't see any way to join the fight in such a way that one side would become friendly to him. Even if he did join in, he wasn't sure how much good this would do. Feudal knights could be thick-armed, thick-headed types who saw any nonknight as dirt beneath their feet, whatever he did for them. Blade didn't plan to end up in some baron's dungeon, suspected of being an escaped serf!

The noise of the fighting seemed to die away as he made his way along the fringes of the village. After a while he left the trees behind and skirted the edge of the grainfields. The grain was as tall as he was, and fortunately hadn't caught fire yet.

Blade was about to head off into the grain, away from the village, when he suddenly stepped out onto open ground. Half a dozen houses straggled out into the fields on either side of a dusty trail. In the middle of the trail, two knights were fighting furiously. Both were on foot and both had blood leaking from their armor, but this didn't seem to be slowing them down much. The green-gloved knight had a morningstar, a spiked ball on the end of a length of chain, attached to a short handle. His black-plumed opponent was wielding a mace and shield.

Blade slipped into one of the cottages and watched the fight from inside its doorway. The knight with the morningstar seemed to have a slight edge. At least he was slowly backing his opponent toward Blade. Blade decided that he might have a good chance after all to make a friend in this Dimension by saving the knight with the mace. Even in the most custom-bound medieval societies, serfs who saved knights were often richly rewarded. Blade sucked at teeth caked with soot and smoke. He decided that for now he'd be satisfied with the reward of a large drink, the answers to a few questions about this Dimension, and no questions asked about himself. He drew his knife and got ready to join the fight.

Then suddenly the whole situation changed. The knight with the mace swung it at his opponent's morningstar as the ball flew toward him. The chain wrapped around the mace, jerking it out of the knight's hand but also immobilizing the morningstar. Before the knight could drop his morningstar and draw his dagger, his opponent ran forward and smashed the steel boss of his shield into the other's face. He crashed backward onto the ground, spitting out blood and loose teeth. His opponent stood over him, placed one foot on his weapon arm, and knelt to finish off the fallen man with his dagger.

The dagger was only inches from the fallen knight's face when a dark shape seemed to fly through the air from the roof of Blade's cottage. It landed on the back of the kneeling knight's neck, and he leaped up with a scream. Then he screamed again and started stabbing futilely at the attacker with his dagger. Blade saw that the animal had a tail, then saw it reach an arm around the helmet. The knight screamed a third time, a horrible shriek of agony and fear, and whirled around. A thin, almost needlelike dagger was sticking out of his right eye. Blade saw that the dagger was smeared with something green and slimy, and realized it was probably poisoned. Then the animal which had stabbed the knight jumped down to the ground and drew all Blade's attention.

It was a living creature, about two feet from head to toe, with a long tail waving behind it. It had roughly the shape and appearance of a Home Dimension monkey, but from where Blade stood it seemed to be entirely covered with feathers. Certainly there were tufts of bright blue-and-green feathers at elbows and knees, and a feather crest on top of its head. It also seemed to be wearing a metal belt of some kind. The whole creature was so unlikely that for a moment Blade wondered if the transition to Dimension X was giving him hallucinations. Then he decided not. The universe was large and strange, and it was never wise to say that something was impossible. If he saw a combat-trained monkey with feathers, he'd assume it was really there.

The stabbed knight staggered about for a minute, screaming, then moaning, then drooling silently. Finally he collapsed, his face turning a sickly yellow, and went into convulsions. By the time he lay still, his opponent was sitting up, exploring his ruined mouth with one hand while the other hand fumbled for his fallen weapon.

He stood up abruptly as he caught sight of the monkey and backed off several steps. It looked to Blade as if he wanted to keep his distance from the monkey, even if it had killed his enemy. The monkey ignored him, scampered over to the dead knight, and began tugging at his dagger. The knight took another step backward. As he did so, he caught sight of Blade standing in the doorway of the cottage.

His response was simple and straightforward. He snatched up his morningstar, whirled it around his head, and charged at Blade.

The monkey's response was just as simple. It forgot about its dagger, leaped into the air with a *yeeeep* of fear, and came down running. Blade didn't see where it went after that. He was too busy with the knight.

Blade would have faced the knight with only his commando knife except for one piece of luck. As the knight swung his morningstar, the mace untangled itself from the chain and flew straight at Blade. He ducked, then caught it almost before it hit the ground. By the time the knight was within striking distance, Blade was ready to meet him.

Blade decided against fighting inside the cottage, although in there the knight wouldn't be able to swing the morningstar. That way he'd lose any claim to honorable treatment. The knight would probably just call up his friends and have Blade butchered on the spot like a wild

22

boar. Instead, he charged out of the cottage door, moving sharply to the right. The spiked ball of the morningstar promptly whizzed past his ear. The knight's wounds seemed to be affecting his accuracy but not his strength. If that ball connected . . .

Blade made two complete circles around the knight, willing to trade a little time for more knowledge of his opponent. The knight had armor and Blade had none. He'd be lucky to get more than one good chance at the man.

At last Blade saw that the knight tended to aim low. He dropped into a crouch, then leaped aside as the ball swept down and bounced violently off the hard-packed earth. For a moment the morningstar was out of control and the knight stood wide open. Blade closed, slammed one hand up under the knight's right arm, and swung the mace hard at the knight's temple. Blade felt sharp edges on the armor gouge his hand, but he also heard metal crunch under the mace. The knight toppled sideways in a cloud of dust and a clattering of armor.

Although blood was running from his nose and ears as well as his mouth, the knight was still breathing steadily. Blade dragged him into the cottage, roughly bandaged his face wounds with clothing torn from his dead opponent, and left him there. At least he'd be out of the sun and not likely to get trampled by stray horses. With luck, someone from his own side would find him before the battle ended. In any case, he wouldn't be talking to anyone until Blade was long gone from this village.

The thought of stray horses reminded Blade that there might be quicker ways of getting out of the village than walking. Getting out of the village quickly was now even more important than before. The screams of the poisoned knight must have made enough noise to be heard all over the village. Someone would investigate before too long.

Blade found a horse with black plumes on its bridle tethered behind the third cottage along the trail. He approached it cautiously, remembering that a knight's trained war-horse was sometimes a one-man animal. At best it would be highly suspicious of strangers, although Blade trusted his horsemanship to keep him in the saddle if the horse let him mount at all.

Blade was standing quietly in front of the horse, letting it get used to his scent, when a feather-monkey darted around the end of the cottage and dashed under the horse's belly. It leaped high, stabbing with its dagger, and as it came down it rolled out from under the horse. The horse reared with a scream of pain and surprise. Blade jumped back as the horse reared again, waving its forefeet and snapping its teeth in his face. It reared a third time, the railing to which it was tethered snapped like a rotten twig, and it bolted. The feather-monkey jumped up and down, squealing and squeaking in triumph.

That was its last mistake. Blade swung the mace, then threw it as hard as he could. It was as accurate as the commando knife, which wasn't designed for throwing, and much heavier. It caught the monkey across the back. The triumphant squealing turned to a pitiful *yip-yip-yip* which went on until Blade ended it with his knife.

This was the second time in less than twenty minutes that he'd seen one of those feather-monkeys show training or possibly even intelligence. It was better to assume that the monkey who attacked the horse could also warn its human masters about Blade. By killing it he'd gained another few minutes head start.

Blade used a couple of those minutes to make a quick search of the nearest cottage. Between the villagers carrying off their valuables and the knights looting everything else, there wasn't much left. He did find half of an old blanket, a cracked bow with a still-sound bowstring, and a foot-long chunk of sausage which smelled fresh.

Outside again, he wrapped the dead monkey in the blanket and tied it up with the bowstring. Then he stuck the sausage in his belt, sheathed the knife, and started off down the trail at the mile-eating lope he'd learned from the warriors of Zunga.

Five minutes later, six knights rode in among the cottages. They were too far away for Blade to make out which side they were on, and they showed no signs of seeing him. By then he was far enough away that they probably took him for one more stray villager, not worth chasing down.

Chapter 5

Fields and orchards stretched out for miles around the village. Beyond them to the east lay a range of rugged wooded hills. Blade headed for these hills, which offered the best cover in sight.

By the time he reached them it was late afternoon. Several times he'd had to turn aside or hide to avoid being discovered by bands of roughly clad men and women. If they were all refugees from the village, most of its people must have escaped before the two bands of knights started fighting up and down its streets. Blade only hoped they would have homes to return to, instead of heaps of smoking ashes.

From halfway up the side of the first hill, Blade looked back to the village. The smoke from the burning houses now formed a dark pillar, miles high. On either side of the pillar, he saw the glint of sunlight on armor as the two bands of knights marched off. He saw one band heading almost straight toward him and decided to get farther into the hills before they arrived.

As he scrambled across the rocky, brush-grown slopes, he had time to bless the sandals Lord Leighton's new invention let him wear. His feet were tough as leather, but on this kind of ground even he couldn't move as fast as he wanted.

At sunset Blade sat under a tree and looked down at a winding pass through the hills as a party of the green-gloved knights passed. He counted about eighty of them. All were dust-coated and looked weary, some wore bloody bandages, and a few were riding double on lathered horses.

He also counted about thirty squires or servants, wearing boiled-leather jackets and light helmets. They guided pack horses carrying baggage, half a dozen women prisoners, and at least twenty of the feather-monkeys. Without the feather-monkeys, Blade might have wondered if he hadn't traveled into the past instead of into Dimension X. There was nothing else about the cavalcade that would have raised eyebrows in fourteenth-century Europe.

They stopped at a stream less than a hundred yards down the slope from Blade to water their horses. They also transferred some of the monkeys to a single packhorse. Then half a dozen knights with comparatively fresh mounts rode back toward the village, leading the horseload of monkeys. By the time this patrol or rear guard was out of sight, the main body was also on the march again. Blade waited until they were both gone, then slipped down the hill to the stream and drank. When he was no longer thirsty, he filled his canteen and scrambled back up the hill into the trees until the pass was a good mile away. The pass and the stream would naturally draw anyone on the move tonight. Blade wanted to sleep undisturbed, then worry about getting to know the people of this Dimension in the light of day.

He found a place where at least none of the rocks had sharp edges or points and made himself as comfortable as he could. He also made a mental note that one of the first new pieces of equipment for the next trip would be a sleeping bag or at least a sleeping pad. There was no good reason for losing sleep unnecessarily, no matter how tough you were.

After a couple of bites of the sausage, he decided that could also wait until daylight. The sausage seemed to be one of those preserved foods which never quite goes bad but never tastes very good either.

By now it was completely dark. He lay down again, curled up into a tight ball like a cat, and drifted off to sleep.

Blade woke once during the night, thinking he heard a distant clanging of weapons on armor. It faded so swiftly that he couldn't be sure. After listening briefly to a silence broken only by night birds and the breeze in the treetops, he went back to sleep. When he woke again, it was the dawn of a fine summer day.

The first thing he did was eat some more of the sausage. He was now hungry enough to ignore its taste, if not to actually enjoy it. The second thing was to examine the corpse of the feather-monkey.

This told him some things he hadn't known before, if not as much as he wanted to know. The feathers were definitely a natural growth, not a garment or a graft. They also showed signs of careful clipping and grooming. Otherwise there was nothing extraordinary about the creature. Its eyes were so large that it was probably at home in the darkness almost as much as in daylight. The forehead also looked higher than Blade remembered seeing in most primates, which hinted at a larger brain. That was no more than a possibility, however, and even if the brain was larger that didn't mean intelligence. He hadn't seen the monkeys do anything which couldn't be the result of very careful training. That didn't make them any less dangerous, since they were small targets, they moved fast, and with those poisoned daggers, they only had to reach you once.

Since the dead monkey was beginning to smell, Blade left it under a tree and walked downhill toward the pass. His first sight when he reached it was a dead horse, lying with its head in the stream and flies buzzing around its hindquarters. It showed no signs of any wounds. Blade only hoped it was dead from exhaustion rather than from a poisoned stab by one of the feather-monkeys. As he walked up the pass, he studied every bit of cover large enough to hide a man or even a monkey.

Before he'd gone half a mile, he came to an even less welcome sight. A naked woman lay sprawled on her back beside the trail. She'd died from having her throat cut, but she must have been already half-dead from mass rape before the knife went in. Blade picked her up and carried her into the trees where she could at least lie unseen. The ground was much too rocky for burying anyone with no tools but bare hands and a fighting knife.

He was even more watchful after he returned to the trail. He also wished he had a long-range weapon, perhaps

27

the crossbow he'd mentioned to Lord Leighton. Of course nothing short of a machine gun would do justice to his feelings toward the gang rapists. But that would never be a practical weapon to take into Dimension X. It would be useless as soon as the ammunition ran out, and it would be far beyond local technology in most Dimensions.

Blade didn't worry about changing Dimensions by introducing new technology. He did that all the time, either to save his own skin or sometimes to solve a problem which had to be solved if the people of the Dimension were to survive. He did worry about getting rounded up and perhaps burned at the stake as a sorcerer, for bringing something so advanced the people would call it magic.

The pass and its trail zigzagged back and forth so much that he found himself covering at least four miles on foot for every mile he advanced in a straight line. He'd started early in the morning, but it was past noon before he reached the top of the pass. The trees and boulders on either side made it a perfect place for an ambush. Blade therefore approached cautiously, looking for a stream. It was a hot day and he looked forward to a long, cool drink of water, rather than sipping sparingly from his canteen.

Then he heard the sounds of a battle from the far slope. A man was shouting, more in rage or pain than in fear, weapons were clanging on rocks, and feather-monkeys were chattering and squeaking furiously. He left the trail and cut through the underbrush until he could see down the trail beyond the top of the pass.

A green-gloved knight sat against a tilted slab of rock, his broadsword in one hand and his other arm bleeding and apparently useless. There was more blood on one leg. Just beyond the reach of his sword, three of the feather-monkeys were jumping up and down. A fourth lay twitching on the path, cut in half. Every so often, one of the feather-monkeys would dart toward the knight, then jump back unharmed as he slashed at it.

Blade wondered why one of them didn't climb up on top of the rock slab and jump down. Perhaps it was too smooth or too high? Certainly this wouldn't make any difference in the end. The knight couldn't stay lucky forever. One of the monkeys would reach him with its poisoned dagger, and

28

that would be the end for him, even if he killed the monkey. Or the monkeys might go on taunting him until he collapsed from exhaustion and loss of blood, then move in for an easy kill. Blade decided he was going to save the knight. Whether or not he got an introduction to the local nobility out of it, he couldn't leave the man to be killed.

The first thing to do was cut down the odds. He wasn't going to risk his bare legs against all three monkeys at close range. He searched the ground, looking for a proper stone. When he found one, he crept down to within easy throwing range, judged the distance carefully, then sprang up and threw.

At his public school, Blade was the best bowler on the cricket team. The stone hit the nearest monkey in the head, splattering its brains. The other two monkeys leaped into the air in surprise and fright. One of them came down within reach of the knight's sword. A desperate slash cut off both legs; a second slash cut off its head. Then Blade ran toward the third monkey, to draw it away from the knight.

He succeeded, but almost got himself killed. The third monkey had a diabolical skill at guessing where Blade's legs would be. Several times he had to leap desperately to avoid being stabbed, without time to watch his footing. On the rocky, sloping ground, he knew this meant a fall sooner or later. That might give the feather-monkey all the time it needed.

The strange, almost unnatural duel between the two-foot monkey and the six-foot man went on. Blade realized that he might be able to keep moving until the monkey got tired and slowed down, or lure it within range of the knight's sword. Or perhaps, if he fell deliberately, catching the monkey off its guard . . . ?

Yes.

He waited until he and the monkey circled around each other again, and he was facing downhill. Then he pretended to have a rock slide out from under his foot. He went down on his back, using all his unarmed-combat skill to land unhurt, but still bruising and gouging himself from shoulders to buttocks. The knight roared a curse and the feather-monkey leaped forward with a squeal of triumph. The green-slimed dagger gleamed repulsively in its paw.

29

Then Blade's arm whipped forward and a handful of gravel hit the monkey like the blast from a shotgun. It wasn't seriously hurt, but it squealed and closed its eyes for a moment, without jumping back out of Blade's reach.

That was all he needed. He foot shot out and took the monkey in the ribs. It flew into the air like a mortar shell with a squeal of pain and terror, traveled at least fifty feet, bounced twice, and lay still.

Blade got up, made sure the knight was fit to be left alone for a little longer, and walked down to make sure the monkey was dead. It was. He felt none of the triumph or even the satisfaction he usually felt after winning a fight. As dangerous an opponent as the monkey was, there was something disgusting about a fight with such a small creature.

By the time he returned, the knight was struggling to get to his feet. Blade reached out a hand to help him up. Instead of taking a firm grip, the knight jerked his own good hand back and picked up his sword.

"You are no Lord from the Lands of the Crimson River," he said sharply, giving the tall, half-naked stranger in front of him the once over. "And I gave you no permission to touch me."

Blade frowned. "You can hardly——"

"Nor did I give you permission to speak. That is two offenses against a Lord to your name. If you will tell me what that name is, I may ask that your punishment be light. If you commit the third offense of trying to conceal who you are, I can have no mercy. Nor would I wish to." He laid his sword across his knees.

Blade was already tired, hungry, thirsty, sore, and angry over the fight with the monkey. The knight's arrogance was the last straw. "I don't need your mercy," he snapped. "You can save it for those who need it, like yourself. You're tired, you're wounded, and there may be more of those damned monkeys around. You'll be very lucky to reach home without help, and frankly I don't much care if you do. If you're an example of a Lord, then no man in his right mind could want to be one!"

The Lord's head jerked back at Blade's words, as if the Englishman had slapped him. Then he bowed his head on his chest and laid his sword down. Tonelessly he mumbled, "I have spoken words against the honor of a Lord. I have spoken words against the honor of a Lord. I have spoken words against the honor of a Lord." He raised his head and looked at Blade. "You have the right to challenge me when I am fit to fight. You might even have the right to leave me here to die, for I—"

"I'm not leaving you here to die," said Blade. "Forget that idea right now." It was the first thing he could think of, and he said it mostly so that his confusion wouldn't show on his face. From fierce arrogance to almost cringing apologies in a moment—was this man mad?

"You do not need to forgive me for not recognizing you until you spoke," said the Lord. "I was taught not to judge a Lord by his garb when I was only twelve. There is no excuse for my forgetting it. None!"

The light dawned in Blade's mind. The society in this Dimension was rigidly divided into Lords and everybody else. The Lords were the masters, their status carefully guarded by laws and customs as well as their own weapons. No non-Lord would dare to talk back to a Lord the way Blade had. Therefore he had to be a Lord, however strangely he was dressed. Sometimes rigid class systems, stupid customs, and narrow minds could be useful.

He laughed. "Indeed I am probably dressed less like a Lord than any Lord you have seen since you were twelve. So I do forgive you for that mistake, now that you have freely admitted it. I have made worse mistakes myself, and have the scars to prove it." Indeed Blade had scars enough to prove almost any story he wanted to tell anyone in any Dimension.

He looked around. "Now—my offer to help you out of here stands. I am more than willing to discuss the mistakes Lords can make with any man, but not here and now. Not when more of those cursed little creatures may appear at any moment." He wasn't sure what the feather-monkey's name was in this land, and didn't want to give himself away by calling them by the wrong one. The computer had done its usual job of altering his brain so that he and the Lord could understand each other, but it never took care of minor details like this.

The Lord sighed and nodded, then let Blade help him up. After a few cautious steps, he found he could walk, leaning on his sword. Blade borrowed the Lord's dagger and cut a crude staff for him from a nearby bush. "I think we'd better keep our weapons ready."

"Very true, although I am not sure the danger is from the Feather People. There shouldn't be any more nearby." He frowned. "But there shouldn't have been any at all, except—" He broke off with a look at Blade, as if he'd just realized he was about to say something a stranger should not hear.

With the staff, the Lord could walk without Blade's help, although not quickly. When they passed the dead monkey Blade had kicked, the Lord stared hard at it and shook his head. "That one—it is hard to say—it looks like one of our own—but that would mean . . . No. It cannot be!"

Blade frowned. "I would not be too sure that in war *anything* cannot be. War is the most uncertain thing men can do."

The Lord frowned. "You talk like a Lord sometimes, but now you do not. It is the purpose of the Lords to make war less uncertain, more fit for men of honor."

Blade resisted the temptation to ask how successful they'd been.

Chapter 6

The trail now lay all downhill, twisting and winding around the usual boulders and outcroppings of rock. With the sun still high overhead, the heat radiating from the rocks was like an oven. Sweat streamed off Blade and he wondered how the Lord stood the heat in full armor. The warrior tramped along, though, and only slowed down when the muscles of his wounded leg began to bind.

After that, Blade had to wonder how much longer the Lord could stay on his feet, and how to offer help to a man with such fierce pride. He also wondered *what* help he could offer. He would find it hard to carry an armored man, but it would do even less good to leave him and search an unknown land for his comrades. He finally decided to start by carrying the man's helmet, and made the suggestion the next time they stopped for rest.

The Lord stared at Blade. "That offer hardly seems fit for you to make. It is certainly not fit for me to accept it. I have offended against your honor so greatly that *I* should be carrying *your* armor. If you wore any," he added. "For you to carry anything of mine now would be doing the work of a Lord's Helper. You are a full-fledged Lord, and—"

Blade held up a hand to stop the torrent of protest which would otherwise probably go on until they both dropped dead of thirst and heat. "Indeed, I am a Lord. Therefore I ask you to listen to me, and believe that I mean nothing against your honor.

"First, there is no one to see us, or at least no Lord who might be a proper witness against us. That I did a Helper's work for you when you needed it done will remain our secret.

"Second, my honor is also at stake here. I must do everything I can possibly do to protect another Lord from danger. Is this not so?"

Reluctantly, the other man nodded. Blade grinned. "I thought so. Now, if I do not carry your helmet, you will be in more danger than you would be otherwise. Therefore I *must* carry your helmet, or my own honor is wounded. Curse it, man—if we faced a battle and I had two helmets while you had none, would you refuse one? This is almost the same case!"

The Lord now seemed to be thinking things over. Blade could almost hear the mental gears turning. Then the Lord nodded slowly and began undoing the laces of his helmet. He said nothing all the while until Blade had the helmet tucked securely under his left arm, and even then he only muttered "Thank you." When they started off again he seemed more determined than ever to keep up the pace until he could no longer walk at all. Blade hoped he wouldn't have to go through this sort of argument over the meaning of honor every time some practical detail came up. Back in Home Dimension, that sort of nonsense helped give "honor" a worse name than it deserved.

Oh, well, he thought. *If I wasn't fairly tolerant of hearing people talk nonsense they'd have locked me up a long time ago!*

By mid-afternoon they'd covered several miles from the top of the pass. Blade's canteen was almost empty, but he saw that the Lord's lips were cracked and dusty and offered him the last of the water. The Lord shook his head. "You are generous, but—no, I am not being foolish by refusing, either. If my eyes still see clearly, we're not more than a hundred paces from a stream."

The Lord's eyes hadn't fooled him. He bent down and drank while Blade kept watch, then did the same while Blade drank. Blade was going on to fill his canteen when they both heard a horse neigh from the bushes just upstream. The Lord started forward. Blade rose to hold him back and the Lord turned to whisper almost fiercely.

"No. There is only so much I can let you do for me. Furthermore, if it is an ambush and I die, you can still escape with a warning. If you die, I cannot move fast enough to get away and warn Lord Alsin and Duke Cyron." He pulled free of Blade's grip with such strength that nothing short of knocking him down could have stopped him. Blade couldn't go that far, and he also knew the man's reasoning made sense. Maybe his obsession with honor hadn't completely wiped out his brains after all!

The Lord disappeared into the bushes; the horse neighed again, then there was the sound of cursing. Blade clapped the Lord's helmet on his head and drew his knife. Then the Lord reappeared, leading a pack horse. The horse was dusty and had several minor wounds, but otherwise looked fresh and healthy. Stuffed into one saddlebag was the body of a feather-monkey, almost black with flies.

The Lord knelt with a disgusted look and pulled the

34

monkey out of the bag. Then he studied the horse. He seemed to recognize it and be looking for something. Finally he turned to Blade, his face suddenly a mask. Blade remembered his examining the feather-monkey at the top of the pass, and how he seemed to recognize that one also.

"I think you see some danger which you did not see before," said Blade. "Is it the same danger you thought of when you looked at the Feather People I killed?" The question was the sort a Lord would ask, and it was also necessary. Blade refused to walk into unknown dangers if there was any chance of learning something beforehand.

The Lord's mask cracked for a moment, and he jerked his head. "That is so. I wish—yet I cannot. I do not even know your name or duchy."

"I am called the Lord Blade," Blade replied. "As for the rest, I have sworn the most solemn and sacred oaths which can be sworn, not to reveal it to anyone save a Duke." He mentally crossed his fingers, hoping this Dimension had such oaths.

Apparently it did. "I am the Lord Gennar, sworn to Duke Cyron of Nainan. Did you swear your oath by the Father of the Crimson River?"

"When I renewed my oaths here in these lands, I swore by him." Blade hoped that would be enough.

Gennar frowned. "Then it will be a crime against both my honor and yours if I ask you to break your oaths, simply to give me peace of mind." He was now sweating from more than the heat. Blade saw the nails of his good hand digging into the palm hard enough to draw blood.

Blade decided to rescue Lord Gennar. "If there is danger close at hand, we will be facing it together. So we must each speak as freely as we can." He pretended to hesitate. "There are some things I can tell you without truly breaking the oath. I think they will be enough for now. If I tell you these things, will you swear to hold nothing back about the danger we face?"

Gennar's breath went out of him in a long sigh. "Yes. By my honor as a Lord and the birthright of Duke Cyron, by the temper of my sword and the cleanness of my blood, I swear to do as you ask."

"That is more than enough," said Blade. "Now—what I

35

can tell you is simple enough. I am from a land so far from the Crimson River that I do not think you would recognize its name even if I was allowed to tell you. If your Duke is a very wise man, he may, but not even most Dukes have heard of my homeland.

"I was a Lord of this land. An accusation was made against my honor. I knew it was false, but I could not prove the falseness without bringing harm to innocent people. So I was sent into exile for the space of ten years, and also made to swear the most terrible oaths which a Lord of my land can swear. While I was in exile, I could tell my story to no one below the rank of Duke. Even then I should tell it only if otherwise I would not be given the treatment proper to a Lord."

"Yes. A Lord remains a Lord, even in such a harsh exile as yours. I think your—Duke?—must have believed you innocent, otherwise he would not have taken such care to guard your honor."

"Perhaps he did. Certainly my enemies were so powerful that he could have done anything else only at the cost of war among his own Lords. Since other Dukes were greedy for his land—" Blade broke off and shook his head. "Forgive me, but I cannot tell you more without breaking my oath."

"I would never ask that," said Lord Gennar, embracing Blade. "I will also say—*I* believe you were innocent. You have done and said things which no man with any blot on his honor could possibly have done or said."

"I thank you," said Blade. "I hope that in these lands of the Crimson River I will do nothing to make you regret those words. Now, I suggest you get on that horse and we continue our journey. I know you have much to tell me, and I will gladly listen. But if there is danger to us, no good will come of staying here and letting it get closer while we talk."

"That is the truth, the Father knows!" said Gennar with a wry grin. With Blade's help he struggled into the saddle and settled in as comfortably as he could. Then Blade took the horse's bridle and led it back onto the trail. He was glad he now had a chance to learn about this Dimension, without having raised any doubts about his being a Lord. In this Dimension his chances of success or even survival would depend on keeping up that masquerade.

All the lands Lord Gennar knew of were divided among two Kingdoms and the seven Duchies of the Crimson River. The two Kingdoms were known only as the East Kingdom and the West Kingdom. Once they'd had other names, but so long ago that nobody living remembered them.

Along the eastern border of the West Kingdom and the western border of the East Kingdom lay mountain ranges, with only a few passes through them. These mountains protected the seven Duchies scattered along the Crimson River, which flowed roughly from north to south. Once the Dukes owed allegiance to one or the other of the two Kingdoms, but they'd been independent for centuries.

The Dukes and the Lords who made up their fighting forces used that independence for continuous petty warfare. Nothing more than a few villages ever changed hands permanently. For many of the Lords the warfare was no more than healthy outdoor exercise and a chance to show off their skill and honor. Many Lords still ended up crippled or dead, though, and of course the loss of life and property among the peasants was heavy. This didn't seem to matter; Lord Gennar actually spoke of the need to keep the peasants too frightened of the Lords to think of rebelling.

The Lords of the Crimson River also knew other ways of wasting their resources. The Feathered People or Feathered Ones had more than an animal's intelligence. Legend and folklore said they'd been discovered long ago, near a great stone that fell from the sky. Blade made a mental note to find out more about these legends. Were the monkeys a mutation, or possibly even from another planet?

The Feathered Ones could be trained for war, to attack horses or even Lords with their poisoned daggers. They could also be trained to fight more formal duels with each other. Enormous sums of money could change hands in bets on these duels. In the last twenty years alone, more than a dozen Lords had been completely ruined through losing bets on monkey duels.

The fighting monkeys were trained to be loyal to their own side. The dueling monkeys were trained, even more thoroughly, to be loyal to their masters and no one else. From Gennar's description, there could sometimes even be something like a telepathic link between a master and his monkey. Such a link was regarded as extraordinary proof that the man stood high in the favor of the Father of the River.

"I begin to understand," said Blade. "The Feathered Ones who attacked you were from your own Duchy?"

Gennar started. "You do not see into other people's thoughts the way one of the Feathered People can, do you?"

"No. I do not think I reveal anything when I say that I have traveled through many lands and fought in most of them. I have seen this sort of thing happen elsewhere. Usually it means there is treachery involved, and sometimes treachery in a place where it is hard to fight it."

"It is just that way here," said Gennar. He went on with his explanation, now talking fast, in jerky sentences with occasional hard looks at Blade. In spite of this nervousness, Gennar told the rest of his story clearly. He was one of the Lords in the patrol Blade saw riding back to the village in the evening. "We wanted to catch the villagers returning with their valuables. We hoped for better loot or at least a few more women. We found only death."

On the way back to the village the pack horse carrying the Feathered Ones broke away and vanished. Just outside the village the Lords were ambushed by a band of the Feathered Ones. Only Gennar and one other Lord got free, and the other Lord was dying from a poisoned dagger slash. Gennar stayed with him until he died, then fought off a band of outlaws and rode up into the pass.

"In the darkness we could not see whose Feathered People our attackers were. We thought they might be of one of our enemies, the Lords of Faissa. Then we found two of ours today where they should not have been, and this horse. I think it is possible that some of our Feathered People were turned against us."

"You say *were* turned? They did not act on their own?"

"All the Fathers forbid! If they are coming to have that

38

kind of will of their own, we are all in danger! No, I think it was our Master of the Feathers. Why, I do not know, and I would rather not speak of what I only suspect. Does this violate my oath?" He looked anxiously at Blade.

Blade shook his head. "No. The Master of the Feathers has so many opportunities for treachery every year that all a man's fingers and toes are not enough to count them. If he is proud or ambitious as well, as they often are . . ." That was as much as he dared say without knowing what a Master of the Feathers was.

"Very true. Not that a Master of the Feathers has no right to pride. He bears a great responsibility, watching over some five hundred of the Feathered People and their work. But I agree—they often think they are worthy of a higher place, and if someone offers it to them in return for a little help . . ."

They moved on in silence. So the Master of the Feathers was a Duke's chief monkey trainer? He certainly would have all sorts of chances for nasty kinds of treachery against anyone he saw as an enemy.

Blade had no doubt the monkey trainer of Duke Cyron would see him as an enemy, the moment word of this day's events got out. The man would have even more chances for treachery against a strange Lord wandering into the duchy from nowhere, one who didn't dare ask too many questions for fear of revealing that he wasn't a Lord at all!

Blade wasn't particularly worried; he'd survived more plots than most men ever read about. But he still knew that during his first few weeks among the Lords of the Crimson River, he'd better walk even more carefully than usual in a new Dimension.

Chapter 7

They reached the camp of Duke Cyron's Lords just before dark. Blade was beginning to wonder if they would be having dinner on what was left of the sausage, then saw the campfires ahead. A moment later he heard a sentry hail them.

"Who goes there?" The almost universal words, which Blade had heard in more lands and Dimensions than he could remember.

"Lord Gennar, the only survivor of Lord Fingo's party. I have with me the Lord Blade, an outlander under oath of secrecy."

This announcement caused a considerable uproar. The sentry ran back into the camp, bawling the news at the top of his lungs. From the camp dozens of men came rushing, some tripping over trailing bootlaces and nearly falling into the campfires. Many were Lords, some were Helpers, and some wore so little it was impossible to guess their rank. Blade also saw half-naked women peering out from the door of a large tent. The uproar and the smell of garbage and open latrines told him that Duke Cyron's army had the usual loose discipline of medieval warriors. In battle they might be hardly more than an armed mob, even if most of the individual Lords in the mob were good fighters.

Eventually a squarely built Lord of medium height pushed his way through the crowd and shouted for silence. Gennar whispered to Blade, "That is Lord Alsin, Marshal to Duke Cyron."

Alsin drove the spectators back with bellowed oaths, but Blade was still aware of curious eyes on him while Alsin and Gennar talked. For the first time since arriving in this Dimension, he wished he had more clothes on. He'd been so glad not to be stark naked that he'd almost forgotten that his present outfit might also look odd.

When Alsin and Gennar were finished, the Marshal turned to Blade and had him tell his version of the day's events. At last Alsin shook his head grimly. "This treachery you both describe means trouble for the duchy, of a kind we have long expected but hoped would not come so soon."

"I am sure I can fight the   " began Gennar.

The Marshal interrupted him. "I am sure you will fight no one for several weeks, and if you will not swear this I will have you tied to your bed!" He lowered his voice, apparently trying to avoid Blade's hearing him. Blade's sharp ears made this futile. He heard the Marshal add, "I ask nothing against your honor, only that you think of more important battles to come." Then Alsin turned to Blade.

"Lord—Blade. You have made a friend of a man more truthful than most, in saving Gennar from—the dangers he faced. I think you also have another Lord in this camp who will speak for you to the Duke. You must be the man who fought Lord Ebass after he'd been wounded."

"The Lord whose opponent was slain by a Feathered One?"

"Yes."

"I am that man," said Blade. "I would not have fought Lord Ebass at all, but he seemed to be leaving me no choice."

"That is so, and he admits it. He also admits that after learning what you must have done afterward, he owes you an honorable forfeit."

"Doubtless we can speak of this when he is healed," said Blade. "He will heal, I hope?"

"Some teeth are gone forever, and he will be muddleheaded for a few days. But otherwise he will heal. Lord Ebass is harder than most to kill," Alsin added wryly. "Now, as for you— I hope I am not speaking too much against your honor when I ask you to give your word that you will not seek to escape. Then you may ride with us as a free Lord to meet the Duke at Castle Ranit. Otherwise . . ."

Alsin's voice trailed off, as if the alternative was too shameful to mention unless Blade forced him to do so.

"I will ride with you, and lift a weapon against no man among you," said Blade. "By the Fathers I swear it. I will even ride with only this knife, if you will swear that no man will be allowed to raise sword against me."

"Most surely I swear it," said Alsin.

"And I will guard—" began Gennar, before a glare from the Marshal silenced him.

"You will guard your tongue before anything else," said Alsin sharply. "I am quite serious about binding you to your bed, if you go on showing no more wit than a boy."

Gennar looked sulky, until Blade gripped him by both shoulders. "Come, my friend. I have put a good deal of work into bringing you home. Don't waste it by not taking proper care of yourself."

There was enough light from the campfires for Blade to see Gennar blushing. "I am sorry," he said. "My tongue is quick, even when my sword cannot be."

Alsin rolled his eyes up to the stars. "To think I've heard him admit it!" He laughed. "All right, Gennar. To the doctors with you. Blade, come with me. Some clothes first, then a meal." Blade followed the Marshal through the crowd, realizing suddenly how good the idea of food sounded.

On the whole, he could be satisfied with his position. Without giving up his masquerade as a Lord, he'd managed to place himself under Alsin's protection. That could give him at least a few days' security against whatever plots might be brewing in the Duchy of Nainan, while he used his own eyes and ears to learn his way around.

Like the Lords themselves, Castle Ranit would have looked at home anywhere in fourteenth-century western Europe. When Blade saw it two days later, silhouetted against the dawn on its hilltop, he again had the feeling he might have traveled in time as well as in Dimensions.

A dry moat protected the castle on three sides. On the fourth side the hill plunged a hundred feet straight down to a meandering tributary of the Crimson River. The castle itself was a huge square, with towers set at intervals around the yellowish stone walls. In the middle a round keep towered at least a hundred and fifty feet, and Blade saw the roofs of outbuildings peeping over the walls all around it. From the flagstaff on the keep streamed Duke Cyron's banner, a clawed green hand on a silver field.

The Lords rode through the village at the foot of the hill at a brisk trot, while chickens, pigs, and small children scurried in all directions. Blade remembered the day before, when he'd seen the Lords gallop through a village and trample a little boy into the mud. He could only grit his teeth and ride on, not daring to help or even rein in. Along the Crimson River those who weren't Lords were expected to get out of the way of Lords. If they didn't, anything that happened to them was their own fault.

The drawbridge across the moat swung down and the riders clattered in through the dark, musty gate into the castle's courtyard. Blade reined in hastily to avoid a stray dog, then two grooms were holding his horse's head so he could dismount. As he did so, he noticed that most of the castle's outbuildings were wood, with thatched or shingled roofs. Even the stone hall with its slate roof had high windows and a wide, unbarred doorway. This castle wasn't expected to stand a full-scale siege. Otherwise the outbuildings would have been stouter, or at least more fireproof.

Alsin led Blade straight into the hall, while the other Lords were still dismounting. The hall was hung with tapestries, some of them explicitly erotic, and crowded with polished wooden furniture. At the far end of the hall stood a chair almost large enough to be called a throne, made of intricately carved stone inlaid with ivory and decorated with gold leaf. On it sat a white-bearded man, who had to be Duke Cyron.

Blade expected heralds to sound trumpets or at least announce names, but Alsin simply strode down the hall toward the Duke. Again Blade followed. If Marshal Alsin didn't know the proper etiquette, no one did. Blade also remembered the casual way the Lords treated each other on the march. Along the Crimson River every Lord was equal to every other Lord. If another Lord's behavior offended you, you either ignored it or challenged him to a duel.

When they reached the throne, Alsin went down on one knee. Blade went down on both knees, figuring that as a complete stranger on parole, he ranked as low as a Lord could. As the Duke exchanged greetings with his Marshal, Blade studied the older man.

The Duke was about the same size and shape as the Marshal, half a head shorter than Blade's six feet one but nearly as broad across the shoulders. He wore a knee-length green robe with red borders over dark blue hose, and the legs inside the hose still showed a good deal of muscle. His head was nearly bald, but a bushy white beard reached down to the middle of his chest. The brown, wrinkled face above the beard was so much like an older version of Marshal Alsin that Blade found himself looking cautiously from one man to the other, making sure the resemblance wasn't just a trick of the light.

It wasn't. If the Duke and his Marshal weren't blood kin, Blade knew he'd like to hear the explanation for their looks. However, he hadn't heard a word on the matter from any of the Lords, who'd been looking at Alsin and the Duke every day for years. If this was one of the things that Nice People Didn't Talk About, then Blade would be one of the Nice People.

The greetings finished, Alsin told the story of the battle and what Blade did. By the time he'd finished, most of the Lords of the war party had crowded into the hall and were listening as intently as if they'd never heard the story before. Blade also noticed that some of them kept looking nervously over their shoulders toward the hall door.

"—like a Lord, so it seemed that his story was worthy of belief," finished Alsin. "Your Grace, I lay the matter of Lord Blade in your hands."

The Duke stared at Blade, who now realized that the man was extremely nearsighted. It didn't affect his dignity, and Blade doubted that it affected much else. He was the sort of man who would look twice as hard to compensate for seeing only half as well!

"Certainly you have the look of a Lord, and I have never known Alsin to be less than truthful. So you shall kneel like a Lord, not like a Helper." Blade cautiously shifted to one knee. "Now, Lord Blade. Tell me the story of your deeds on the day of the battle in your own words, and be brief."

Blade was halfway through his story when a sudden commotion behind him made the Duke look past him toward the door of the hall. Blade turned to see a dark-haired man, who must have been nearly seven feet tall, shouldering his way through the crowd of Lords. As they gave way before him, Blade saw that the man wore a suit of leather and had one of the Feathered People perched on each shoulder. A broadsword dangled from his waist, looking hardly larger than an ordinary man's dagger. Blade didn't need the whispers to tell him that this was Orric, the Master of the Feathers to the Duke of Nainan. He also didn't need Duke Cyron's suddenly frozen face to tell him that right now Orric was about as welcome as a man-eating tiger.

"Who mumbles lies about me into His Grace's ear?" roared Orric. His voice was in proportion to the rest of him.

Before either Alsin or the Duke could speak, Lord Gennar limped out of the crowd. He stood straight, even if he needed the help of a cane to do so. "I say the truth about what happened to me, and I would not have lived to tell of these things save for Lord Blade," said Gennar firmly.

"I say that what is said against me and my loyalty to Duke Cyron is not true." Orric rested one hand on his sword hilt. "By this steel I swear it."

There was a long silence, and Blade got the distinct impression that everyone was waiting for somebody else to speak. Then Lord Gennar gripped his own sword and drew it.

"By this sword I swear that my words are the truth," Gennar said.

"Then you have spoken words against the honor of a Lord," said Orric, pronouncing the ritual phrase slowly and carefully. Each word was like a stone dropping into a well. He lowered his voice and said almost casually, "*My* honor. I will prove on your body that your words are false."

Blade saw Lord Gennar swallow, but his voice was steady as he replied. "I shall prove upon *your* body that I speak the truth."

45

This time the silence was broken by occasional mutterings. Blade heard the word "champion," and saw a look pass between Alsin and the Duke at the word. Blade drew his knife and took two steps forward.

"I claim right to stand as champion to Lord Gennar. It will be some time before he is fit to fight Orric. Without a champion he must spend all that time bearing the name of 'liar,' or else fight and lose, to meet disgrace as well as death. That will be no true judgment of the Fathers, whatever Orric may have done or left undone."

The Master of the Feathers glared at Blade. "This is no fit champion for Lord Gennar. He is no Lord."

Marshal Alsin's sword was out of its scabbard before the echo of Orric's words died. "He is a Lord, for I have brought him before the Duke as one. He is a fit and lawful champion by the laws and customs of the Duchy of Nainan."

"And I have received him as a Lord," said the Duke, with a sideways look at his Marshal. "Therefore he is a Lord, by my will and judgment. Will you dispute this, in order to pick a fight which will prove nothing but that a healthy man is stronger than a wounded one?"

Blade rather wished the Duke hadn't added the last sentence. From the murmuring it seemed he had the Lords on his side, but Orric was growling like a hungry bear and looked ready to start swinging his sword at any moment. Blade measured the distance to the Master with his eyes, and shifted a couple of steps to the right, to make sure he was between Orric and the Duke. He also hoped Gennar would keep quiet. All they needed to set Orric off now would be another well-intentioned remark from Gennar.

Apparently Orric could also estimate the odds he would face if he openly defied the Duke. He drew his sword and saluted Blade with such elaborate courtesy that it was like a slap in the face. "So be it. If Lord Gennar consents, I shall fight Lord Blade as his champion. Does he consent?"

Gennar's head jerked in an angry nod; apparently he didn't trust himself to speak.

"Very well. I do not imagine that the Lord Blade will have long to enjoy his rank, nor Lord Gennar to enjoy the reputation of a truthful man. But that is as the Fathers will it." He sheathed his sword with more elaborate flourishes, bowed to the Duke, bowed again to all the Lords, and stalked out. Blade noted that in spite of his size he moved with grace and precision.

Then everyone was crowding around, pounding him on the back and shoulders, packed so densely that Gennar with his wounded leg and arm was in danger of being knocked down. Above the close-cropped heads of the Lords, Blade saw Alsin and the Duke exchanging more looks. As soon as he could, he pushed his way through the crowd to Gennar. "I hope I didn't kick you out of the frying pan into the fire by offering to be your champion."

"Out of the—oh, I understand. No. At least I think not. You have put yourself into a bad place, though. Orric will be out for blood, and he has never yet been beaten by any single man. That is why the Duke and Alsin—" He broke off as Blade put a finger to his lips and nodded politely. He would have liked to hear whatever Gennar had to say about the Duke and Alsin, but this wasn't the time or place.

Then Marshal Alsin was shouting in his bull's roar for everyone's attention, and the Lords saw the Duke stand up and draw his dagger. "In all we have just seen, we must not forget that this day we celebrate another victory of Nainan over Faissa. This day and this night we feast, and let no Lord hold back, for you have all deserved well of your Duke."

The cheering echoed around the hall, and Blade saw that his duel with Orric had been completely forgotten. He wasn't surprised. He might be a Lord, but he was definitely a stranger, and no one in Nainan would be much the worse if Orric did hack him to pieces. The thought would have weakened the courage of a man less accustomed than Blade to guarding his own back from all enemies.

47

Chapter 8

With all the people crowded into it, Castle Ranit quickly ran short of hot water for baths. Some Lords were able to bribe a bucket or two loose from the cooks. Blade had no money, and no one was willing to accept his promises to pay. Everyone seemed to expect this would be his last night on earth. He would have gone unbathed and travel-stained to the feast if Lord Gennar hadn't shared his own water.

When Blade stepped into the hall for the feast, he was dressed and looked as much a Lord as anyone else in the hall. He had shed his blue shorts and sandals; the former were starting to chafe, and the latter were inappropriate with the hose and tunic he wore. But he still wore the silver loinguard underneath his Lord's attire. Leighton and J would fume if he didn't return home with that. He found the air heavy with the odor of roast meat, candle wax, wood smoke, unwashed humanity, and heavy perfume. Everywhere, Lords drifted back and forth, most of them holding pewter plates of food and horn mugs, many of them with Feathered Ones perched on their shoulders. Along the walls Blade saw servants running back and forth, with barrels of ale and wine, haunches of smoking meat, and loaves of bread so long it took two men to carry them. In addition to the Lords and servants, Blade counted a number of young women, who seemed mostly concerned with staying out of the Lords' way. Their gowns were either short and cut low, or else long and nearly transparent. Unlike most of the Lords, they were all scrubbed clean. If they hadn't been so blank-faced, they'd have been quite decorative.

Everyone except the girls were trying to talk or even shout at once. The squeaking and chattering of the feather-monkeys, the clatter of knives on pewter, and the raw noise of someone vomiting in a corner added to the din. Blade felt like pulling out his knife and silencing a few of the loudest shouters. Instead he elbowed his way through the crowd until he could reach out and snatch a plate of meat from a passing servant. The Lord who'd been supposed to get the plate swore and glared at him, then seemed to remember that this was the man foolish enough to be fighting Orric tomorrow.

"Enjoy your last meal!" he snarled.

"I'll enjoy it anyway," replied Blade, saluting with his knife before sticking it into the largest chunk of meat. It tasted surprisingly good—a cross between beef and pork, with strong but attractive seasoning. He started looking for a quiet corner to eat his dinner, but didn't expect to find one, since the only spot in the hall free of the general uproar was the Duke's corner.

Cyron was sitting at a small table, flanked by a young man in embroidered robes like his own and another figure wearing a hood. All three had silver plates and cups in front of them. Behind them stood Alsin, wearing full armor except for the helmet. On either side of him was a similarly armored Lord, each carrying a short throwing spear. Behind Alsin and his guards was the stone wall. No one could get within twenty feet of the table without being seen by someone there.

Blade was about ready to leave the hall when he saw Alsin waving at him. He put down his empty plate, straightened his borrowed hose and tunic as well as he could, and walked over.

He was barely down on one knee before Cyron lifted him and offered a cup of wine. It was strong and so sour that he nearly gagged on it, but managed to get it down. "Lord Chenosh, the Lord Blade, who has come among us from a distant land and will fight Orric tomorrow. Lord Blade, Lord Chenosh, son of my son and heir to the Duchy of Nainan."

"I am honored," said Blade. The Duke's teenage grandson rose and held out a long-fingered hand to him. Blade noticed

49

it was his left hand. His right hand was held low and concealed in a mitten of black chain mail.

"I hope you live long enough to enjoy that honor," said Chenosh. "It is ill done, that you must—" The Duke's clearing his throat sounded like a shotgun blast. Chenosh frowned but also fell silent.

"There is no reason I should fear the fight with Orric," said Blade. "Unless his not being here tonight means he is plotting some treachery? I have not seen him, and I should think he is rather hard not to see."

"I should say—so much the better if he is planning some treachery," said the hooded figure in a high, firm voice. "Then he will no longer be a lawful Lord." Two petite, long-fingered hands reached up and threw the hood back. Blade found himself staring at a small round face framed in shimmering red hair, with immense green eyes, a freckled snub nose, full red lips. . . . He forced his own eyes to look elsewhere before he violated good manners by staring at the beautiful young woman.

"There might be two opinions on that, my lady," he said. "One of them is yours, the other is mine. If Orric plans treachery, I am its most likely victim. I will get no benefit from Orric's ceasing to be a Lord if I am dead."

Marshal Alsin looked indignant, the Duke's face was a mask, and Chenosh was obviously trying not to laugh. The silence allowed the girl to reply. "I admit your correction, Lord Blade. I did not think how this matter might seem to you."

"I forgive you," said Blade with a grin, which made Alsin look even more indignant. "Come," said Chenosh. "This will never do. Lord Blade, the Lady Miera, my sister."

"Again, I am honored." Blade saw that both Alsin and the Duke wanted to speak but were held back by his presence. He suspected an old family quarrel, one not to be aired in front of strangers. "But I think I see Lord Gennar wanting to speak to me. With Your Grace's leave . . . ?"

"Certainly. The evening is yet young."

Lord Gennar was nowhere in sight, but he'd saved everyone embarrassment. As Blade turned to go he saw the Duke vigorously pulling the hood back over Miera's head.

He still felt her green eyes following him as he plunged back into the crowd.

Blade hardly enjoyed the rest of the feast. The air grew even hotter and thicker with smells, and the wine was too sweet when it wasn't too sour. As the Lords drank the wine and the beer, their behavior became coarse. Blade saw them tripping servants with platters of food or pouring jugs of beer over their heads. Some Lords dragged serving girls off into dark halls. One Lord shoved a girl facedown into a puddle of grease and meat scraps when she seemed reluctant to go with him. Blade was about to intervene when another Lord came over and tried to claim the girl for his own. For a minute it seemed there was going to be a fight, and most of the people in the hall appeared to be looking forward to the prospect. Then the Duke came over and forced the two Lords to settle the matter by a duel between their Feathered Ones.

Everybody cleared a space for the monkeys, making the crowding in the rest of the hall even worse than before. Blade managed to save his ribs only by pushing back every time someone pushed him. He saw two of the girls in the scanty gowns faint but stay on their feet, held up by the sheer press of bodies.

The two Feathered Ones fought with blunted daggers, but the heat and the wildly cheering crowd put them in a frenzy. They leaped around, stabbing and slashing at each other hard enough to draw blood even with blunted steel. By the time the fight was over, the loser could barely stand. Its master promptly kicked it against the wall hard enough to break its back. It slid down to the floor and lay there, squeaking pitifully. The winner's master put his arm around the girl's waist and led her off. At least he was the Lord who'd wanted to rescue her, not the one who'd pushed her into the grease!

Everyone immediately started discussing the fine points of the fight, ignoring the dying monkey. Again Blade was about to intervene when somebody else did so first. This time it was Miera, who pushed through the crowd with Alsin in hot pursuit, bent down, and cut the monkey's throat with her eating knife. Then Alsin was upon her, his hands hovering within inches of her shoulders. Obviously he would have liked to drag her off or at least read her a lecture, but she *was* his overlord's kin. Rage and frustration fought on his face, until the Duke himself arrived and sent Miera out of the hall.

"That was not well done," said a voice beside Blade. He looked around, to see Lord Chenosh standing quietly with his crippled hand tucked into his belt.

"I suppose not. But I was going to do the same thing."

"Ah. I did not mean Miera's boldness, although it will have everyone talking for a week. I meant Lord Barjom's killing his Feathered One. The Feathered Ones have ways of learning which Lords treat them as animals and which are wiser. It will not be long before Barjom can no longer get a Feathered One, even if the Master of the Feathers—" He broke off as he realized Blade might not care to discuss Orric.

"Never mind," said Blade. "Go on. You're saying things about the Feathered People I haven't heard before. I'd like to know about these things." He laughed at the expression on the boy's face and answered the implied question. "Yes, I'm going to live long enough to use what you tell me."

The boy started talking, sometimes gesturing with his good hand. He was well informed on the history and breeding of the Feathered Ones, or at least Blade thought he was. It was hard to be sure with everyone now talking as loudly as if they were calling hogs. Between the noise, the hot air, and the wine and beer, Blade wasn't sure he caught more than one word out of three.

He knew he'd been at the feast too long when someone handed him a silver wire basket of engraved golden balls and he thought they were ripe fruit. He was trying to bite into one when the laughter of the people around him made him realize his mistake. He held up the ball, saw the number "Seven" in fancy script on it, then put it back in the basket.

By then the crowd was beginning to thin out, as people drifted away or collapsed in corners to sleep off their food and drink. Blade got back to the room he was sharing with Lord Gennar to find his roommate gone. An empty leather wine bottle and a discarded woman's dress told how Gennar had spent the evening in spite of his wounds. Blade started discarding his own clothes, and was already naked when he heard a knock. He picked up his knife and crossed to the door.

"Lord Blade?" came a female voice from outside.

"Yes?"

"You drew the Golden Seven, didn't you?"

"The Golden—?" he began, then remembered the golden balls he'd thought were fruit. "Yes, I did."

"I am Seven."

"Then come in, Seven." He opened the door and admired the girl as she stood silhouetted against the torchlight from the hall outside. It was easy to admire her, since she was in one of the semitransparent gowns. She was a little on the thin side, but her breasts were full and firm, and both the hair on her head and the hair between her thighs was a rich curly brown. The only thing spoiling the picture was her eyes, which refused to meet his. In the end he had to practically drag her inside and close the door behind her.

In the process her gown was ripped at the shoulder, so it slid down and lay around her feet. Although the night was warm, the girl started shivering. Blade wished she'd stop. The last thing he felt like doing was making love to a girl who was obviously scared half out of her wits. He sat down on the bed. "Well, Seven. Why are you here?"

The question startled her so, that for the first time she actually looked at him, dark eyes widening. "You—you are one for boys? Oh, my Lord, I beg your pardon. Please, don't beat me for saying that. I have spoken—" She could not go on, and Blade had to grip her hard to keep her from throwing herself on the floor and kissing his feet.

"You have *not* spoken words against the honor of a Lord. I am not a lover of boys, but it was a question you had every right to ask. *I* say you had the right, and no one else can say anything to either of us while we are here tonight!"

"Then—I may stay?"

"You certainly may."

"Thank you. Thank you." She fell on her knees and started kissing him—not his feet, but other and more sensi-

53

tive parts of his body. She worked with a desperation which almost repelled him, but also with a skill which aroused him in spite of himself. At last there was nothing for him to do but bury his fingers in her hair and let her finish what she'd begun. Then his release came, and when he had control of himself he bent down, picked her up, and carried her to the bed. She looked nervously up at him as he laid her down.

"Lord Blade?"

"It's your turn now."

"My—turn?" She sounded both interested and frightened at the same time.

He didn't bother trying to explain. He suspected that she'd never met a man who had any thought for her pleasure as well as his own. He bent over her, kissing her lips until they opened, warm and wet under his. At the same time one hand was stroking the side of her throat and the other the inside of one thigh. Then he moved his lips down her neck, along her shoulder, and down on to a breast, where he spent a long time on the nipple. . . .

By then he knew she was enjoying the new experience. Her breath was coming fast, and every so often she gave a little moan. Since he doubted he'd ever be seeing "Seven" again, Blade now set out to give her at least one experience she'd never forget. He put more care and effort into his lovemaking than he'd done at times when his life or manhood depended on pleasing his partner. He still enjoyed every minute of it, and so did "Seven."

At last he let her take him into herself. By then she was hot and wet, utterly willing, utterly ready. Her thighs locked around him, holding him, drawing him on into her, while her hands clawed at his back until her nails broke the skin. Her breath in his ear was almost a roar, and she was fighting not to scream.

Then she did scream, and he felt her spasms spread from deep inside her all through her body. With his manhood buried in the heart of that spasm, there was nothing he could do but follow her. The girl hardly noticed his weight falling on her; she was still shaking and whimpering and sobbing quietly. After what seemed like a long time, Blade found the strength to roll off her. He wrapped her up in his blanket and held her down gently but firmly when she tried to get up and go. After a little while longer, she fell asleep.

Blade knew that tomorrow might really be the last day of his life, in spite of all the confidence he'd shown. If it was, he could at least be sure that he'd spent his last night well.

Chapter 9

The girl woke Blade well before dawn, and they made love again. By the time he'd seen her safely out, there was no point in going back to bed. Although his duel with Orric wasn't planned until late afternoon, in order to let all the Lords in the neighborhood reach the castle, he couldn't spend the day twiddling his thumbs.

Blade wanted to pick his weapons carefully. He had his commando knife, of course, but perhaps he could arrange a surprise or two for his opponent, and that would take time. Even though Duke Cyron had opened the castle's arsenal to him, some of the men in the arsenal were likely to be part of Orric's faction, ready to carry tales to their master. He had a breakfast of stale cheese and weak beer, and was at the door of the arsenal before the sunlight touched the Duke's banner on the castle's keep.

Inside was a treasure house of weapons, enough to make any Home Dimension museum curator drop dead of sheer joy. Blade quickly ruled out the lances, spears, morning-stars, and maces as possible weapons for the duel. The lances were for fighting on horseback, and the duel would be on foot. The spears were for hunting or for the Duke's picked guardsmen. The morningstars were no good for defense, and Blade didn't want to use that sort of weapon against a man with Orric's speed and strength. None of the maces would be long enough against Orric's greater reach.

That left him with his choice of about two hundred swords. One thing Blade could tell at a glance: this was a Dimension where swords were for slashing. For thrusting from horseback they had the lances, for close-in work they had daggers. For everything in between, a Lord slashed or swung rather than thrust. So if he could find a sword which could be given a point before this afternoon, he'd have a real advantage over Orric.

He started examining the swords one at a time, testing them for balance and trueness, bending them to check the temper of the metal, examining the hilts and guards for sound welding. If he couldn't make a thrusting sword to surprise Orric, he at least wanted the best possible conventional weapon.

He was examining what must once have been a two-handed sword with a basket hilt when he heard soft footsteps behind him. He stepped back as he turned, then recognized Lord Chenosh.

The boy held out his good hand in a placating gesture and smiled.

"I'm sorry. I should have remembered that before a duel even the bravest Lord is likely to jump at shadows. I just wanted to get a closer look at that sword."

Blade held out the weapon and Chenosh nodded. "I thought so. You don't want that one. It was used as a roasting spit for a few years, and I don't think its temper is much good anymore. I can't understand why the Master of the Steel keeps it around at all." He pointed at a sword two racks to the left. "Now that one I know is still sound, although you may find it a little heavy in proportion to its length. Since you don't know how much armor you'll be wearing, you—" He went on cataloging the strengths and weaknesses of various swords for quite a while. The absence of bows and arrows, he explained, was the result of a taboo on using archery against men of lordly rank.

Blade listened, trying not to look too surprised, and when Chenosh paused for breath, he nodded. "You seem to know the history of all the weapons in the castle."

The boy flushed and his blue eyes went hard. "The history, yes. The use, no."

Blade realized his mistake. The boy must have heard sarcastic remarks about his crippled hand since he'd reached the age where his healthy comrades were learning sword work.

"I'm sorry," said Blade. "I didn't mean that the way it sounded."

The boy stared for a moment, then said slowly, "I believe you. Mostly because, other than Alsin, you're the first Lord to apologize for saying—that sort of thing." He hesitated, looked around the room, then lowered his voice. "Lord Blade, may I propose a bargain?"

There was no point in being rude to the boy by refusing to hear him. "If this bargain doesn't require me to do anything against my honor as a Lord, I will consider it. Also, I will not go against any plans your grandfather and Lord Alsin have for me."

Chenosh's eyes widened. "You know they have plans?"

"Yes. It's as plain as their beards, to someone who has traveled as much as I have."

"You do not know what those plans are, though?"

"No."

"Then I cannot tell you. But I can swear by my own honor and blood, that what I am asking of you is nothing against Duke Cyron or Lord Alsin. Is that enough?"

"It's enough to make me keep silent about your bargain, even if I don't accept it. Now—what do you want?"

"You are looking for a sword with a point, aren't you?"

Blade decided telling the truth was the best course of action. "Yes. Or at least one which will take a point."

"I thought so. I have read of such swords in the days of the Kingdoms, but no one makes them or uses them now. I will not tell anyone of your plan, even if you refuse my bargain. Believe me, Orric is no friend to me or—" He broke off in the way Blade now knew too well.

Blade sighed. "Will you please tell me what you want? If you can help me, well and good. If you can't, I have a good deal more I must do before this afternoon."

"I will give you all my knowledge of the swords here. I will also lead you to a blacksmith who will work on your chosen sword and keep his mouth shut. In return, you will teach me the art of fighting with a pointed sword. With my hand, I cannot use a regular broadsword and shield. But I could use a small shield and a sword with a point."

Blade looked Chenosh over carefully. He was thinner than most of the Lords, but he seemed to have plenty of well-toned muscle. They'd have to work out a few times before he could be sure, but Chenosh might be the kind of tough, wiry—

"I will not come to your bed, Lord Blade, even if you are a man for men. That would be against my honor and that of the Duchy of Nainan. If you look at me again that way I shall have to tell my grandfather."

Blade mentally counted to ten, then to twenty. By the time he'd finished counting, he could speak quietly. "I was not looking at you with desire. I was looking at you to see if you were the kind of swordsman who could learn to use speed in place of strength. Not everyone can do that, and I would not give you any false hopes."

Chenosh turned even redder than before, and looked at the floor. Blade waited until his face returned to its normal color and he could say, "I am sorry, Lord Blade. I have heard too many of the wrong words, so I have come to expect them even where they do not come. Around you, perhaps I will learn to listen."

"You'd better, if you want my teaching to be any good to you," said Blade flatly. Then he smiled. "I do think you will make a good fencer, or at least one worth teaching. I accept your bargain. Now it's my turn to listen while you show me swords."

Chenosh swallowed and began to point out possibly useful weapons, although it was a while before his voice was completely steady again.

The sun was still high when Blade stepped out into the castle courtyard for the duel. It was hot, with the castle walls shutting off every last breath of wind. The crowd in and around the courtyard made it even hotter. Every bit of wall, every window, and every square foot of ground except the space he and Orric would need for fighting was packed. Blade saw jugs of wine passing around, and in the

58

shade of the wall a few people were already lying sprawled, overcome by the heat or the wine.

Half a dozen of Alsin's chosen Lords were keeping the fighting square clear with drawn swords. The square was no more than thirty feet on a side, but that didn't bother Blade. He would need room only while he was testing Orric's reach and speed, and learning if he had any bad habits or serious weaknesses. After that he wouldn't need much room or much time either, to finish the fight one way or another.

In some Dimensions Blade would have tried to exhaust an opponent of Orric's size and strength until he slowed down. In this Dimension that was considered unlordly, almost cowardly. On the other hand, any trick which still required the courage to stand up to your opponent was all right.

Blade advanced to the center of the fighting square and raised his sword in salute to the crowd around him. The gesture drew a buzz of approving comment. He listened carefully for any remarks about his sword but heard none. The disguise on the point seemed to be working.

It had taken the blacksmith two hours to grind the point on the sword, and another hour to shape the lead foil hiding it. The foil also gave the sword the same balance it had originally, so Blade didn't have to take extra time practicing. The sword still had most of its edge, so if Orric's armor offered him no openings for thrusts, he still had a usable broadsword.

In addition to his sword Blade carried a round shield of wood covered with leather, and the combat knife he had brought with him from Home Dimension. He wore the usual open-faced helmet, plate greaves over leather breeches, and his wire loinguard. His borrowed mail coat only came down to mid-thigh, but it let him move freely. Worn over a leather vest and a quilted arming doublet, the armor already had him sweating heavily, but the undergarments were necessary to keep Orric's blows from driving the rings of the mail into his flesh.

The buzz and mutter of voices swelled as the head of Blade's opponent appeared above the crowd. He pushed his way through to the square, other people making a path for

59

him as fast as they could. Orric wore a longer mail coat but no greaves. He carried a shield and broadsword, and had a double-bitted battle-ax slung across his back. Blade was delighted to see the ax. It confirmed Orric's reputation for liking to make spectacular kills. If he could be tempted into using the ax, a two-handed weapon which gave him little defensive power . . .

Two can play at the game of spectacular kills, my friend Orric.

Duke Cyron stepped into the fighting square. His high-pitched voice rose as he proclaimed the lawfulness of the duel, the names of the opponents, the rules and conditions, and much else that Blade already knew. He kept his face straight and stared at Orric, who was doing a little shuffling dance and waving his sword as the Duke spoke. He was also staring at Blade with naked hatred.

At last Alsin stepped into the square, holding a spear high, and the Duke stepped out. Alsin held the spear out between the two men, and Orric stopped dancing and stepped back. Blade wiped sweat off his face with the back of his hand, then raised his shield and laid his sword across the top of it.

"In the name of the Father of the River, Duke Cyron, and the lordly tradition of honorable combat—Lord Blade and Lord Orric, laaaay *on!*" Alsin sprinted for the edge of the square as the two fighters charged each other.

Orric began striking the moment Blade was in range, and he wasn't trying to test his opponent; he was trying to kill. Each blow crashed against Blade's shield with bone-jarring strength. Orric didn't seem interested in learning his opponent's weaknesses and strengths. He was too confident of his own superiority.

Blade knew that sort of confidence was usually a weakness, and he was an expert at taking advantage of it. Still, Orric was hitting so hard that if many blows did get through Blade's defenses, Blade might be in serious trouble. So he settled down to fight a defensive battle, receiving each blow on his shield, taking the time to learn Orric's other weaknesses.

He quickly learned that the man didn't seem to have any, apart from being a trifle slow. That wasn't likely to give Blade much advantage, since Orric was not only a foot taller but was long-armed even for his height. He had too much of an edge in reach to let Blade get inside his guard without being badly hit on his way back out.

So the duel settled down to an endurance contest, to see which would fail first—Orric's sword arm or Blade's shield. It was hard to tell, although everyone around the square kept shouting guesses. At least Blade didn't hear anyone criticizing him for his ability to stand on the defensive.

Around and around the fighters went, kicking up the dust and rotten straw, tramping the exposed ground hard as stone. Blade saw his opponent's leggings turning dark and felt his own arming doublet getting as soggy as if he'd fished it out of a river.

Once he thought Orric was slowing down and tried a cut at his left knee. The lead-sheathed tip of his sword gouged the sweat-darkened leather. A bare point might have done damage. Orric's reply was so fast and so hard that for a moment Blade lost feeling in his shield arm. He hastily backed clear and kept Orric's sword in play with his own until his shield arm was fit again. Sparks flew each time the two swords crossed, but Orric seemed to take this new technique in his stride. Blade hoped his sword wouldn't lose its edge, strength, or concealing foil tip.

The fight went on until Blade saw shadows creeping across the courtyard. The sun was beginning to set, and light conditions would soon become uncertain. That would give an advantage to Orric, who knew the ground better than Blade. Orric was definitely losing more speed now, but still not enough to offset his longer reach. He'd gambled on a quick victory, but he hadn't risked more than he could afford to lose. The crowd was almost silent now, except for an occasional shout or hiss of breath. Once Blade heard clearly: "No one's stood this long against Orric since he was twenty."

Blade wasn't sure how much longer he could stand. His shield arm seemed to be weighted with lead, and his shield was almost useless. The leather covering hung in strips where it wasn't ripped completely off, exposing bare wood. When Orric's sword smashed into the wood now, splinters flew off hard enough to sting Blade's skin. He laughed grimly at the thought of losing the fight and his life because a splinter hit him in the eye!

The shield wasn't going to last much longer, and when it broke, Orric would almost certainly switch to his ax. If Blade could get rid of the shield at a time of his own choosing, he'd have more control over what followed. He moved forward and to the left, almost jumping in spite of his weary legs. Orric's sword slashed down, sinking into the top of his shield, cutting halfway down to Blade's arm. At the same moment Blade reached out as far as he could and slashed Orric's left leg.

Orric shouted, more in surprise than pain, although the wound was deep enough to bleed freely. All around the square the cry rose: "First blood, first blood to Blade! First blood!"

Alsin stepped forward and shouted for silence. "Blade has first blood," he said briskly to Orric. "Do you wish to yield, as is your right?"

Orric shook his head and growled something Blade didn't catch. Seeing the expression on the man's face, there was no need to hear his words. Blade shrugged his useless shield off his left arm, flexed some life back into the muscles, and drew his knife. Except for his sword arm, there was no longer any part of his body which didn't feel drained and sore. Even his head seemed to be stuffed with cotton wool, and his mouth was full of hot sand.

Then Orric dropped his shield, unslung his ax, and charged.

The ax leaped high and flashed down three times, each time so fast that Blade barely got clear. He knew if that ax ever struck, he'd be dead. But Orric's leg wound was now visibly slowing his footwork, as the ground at his feet turned into red mud. Blade stepped out of range, and raised both sword and knife in what looked like a salute. With a deft movement of his left hand, he thrust the knife point in under the lead foil covering and stripped it free of the sword. The fading sunlight caught the polished metal of the sharpened sword point, but no one seemed to notice.

Certainly Orric didn't. He swung his ax again as his opponent closed. This time Blade went down on one knee as he came within reach. His left hand thrust the knife upward, striking at Orric's armpit, drawing his attention, and diverting the ax swing. The ax handle glanced off Blade's helmet and bruised his shoulder, while the deadly steel head sank deep into the ground. For a second Orric and his weapon seemed to form a single frozen statue. That was enough for Blade to thrust his sword up into Orric's unprotected chin. The sharp point vanished into the flesh, and with all his strength behind it, shot straight up into the brain.

A gurgle came out of Orric's open mouth, then a spray of blood. His eyes stared wildly, then the life went out of them. Another moment and his limbs received their last message from his destroyed brain. He fell backward so violently he jerked the sword out of Blade's hand, landed with a thud and a clang of armor, and lay still, a pool of blood widening around his head. Blade retrieved his sword, raised it in salute, and stepped back from the body.

Chenosh was the first of the crowd to move. He dashed up with a bucket of water, and Blade snatched it as if it were the only thing standing between him and sudden death. Half of it went down his throat so fast he nearly choked. Then he poured the other half all over his face and down his neck.

"Blade!" said Chenosh. "Your armor! It will rust!"

Blade looked blankly at him, fighting back the urge to laugh. He suspected that if he started laughing, he might not be able to stop.

No one heard Alsin's voice announcing the end of the duel, Orric's death, Blade's victory, and the proof of Lord Gennar's accusation. Lord Alsin swore afterward, however, that he had said everything he was supposed to, and everyone believed him. Everyone also saw seven Lords push out of the crowd, gather around Orric's body, then lift it in their arms and bear it away. Chenosh's face hardened at the sight and he said loudly enough for Blade to hear:

"That is open defiance of my grandfather. I do not think we have seen the last of Orric's work today. He is the sort of man who will go on biting, like a dead snake."

Blade wasn't paying any attention to the boy. Miera was stepping forward, her face even paler than before and her

63

mouth working. Both her grandfather and Alsin were watching her, but neither of them made a move to stop her. For a moment Blade thought she was going to walk all the way into his arms, but she had more sense. She stopped just out of reach, threw back her head, and smiled. The smile was the most amazing combination of total innocence and complete sensuality he'd ever seen on a woman's face.

Then he couldn't see anything except a sea of heads, hats, and helmets, as a dozen Lords rushed to him and lifted him on their shoulders. All around, people were shouting his name, and as his bearers carried him toward the hall, the people in the windows above began to throw scarves and flowers.

Chapter 10

Blade could have spent the next few weeks going to one feast after another, being fed and wined and plied with women and praise. Defeating Orric made him for the moment the most popular man in the Duchy of Nainan, except among Orric's allies. These were lying low for the moment, although Duke Cyron, Marshal Alsin, and Blade were all sure they would be heard from again.

Meanwhile, Blade found many ways of spending his time.

There was giving Lord Chenosh fencing lessons.

It was an unusually cool morning for early summer along the Crimson River, and the gray sky promised rain later in the day. Blade and Chenosh rode out to the practice field. Not for the first time, Blade noticed how well the youth handled his horse with only one good hand.

Blade also remembered Chenosh's words the first time he praised the young Lord for his skill in riding.

"It seemed to me that because I could not fight I had to do everything else better than anyone else. I do not know if I could have done this if my father had lived. He always felt that a crippled son and a proud daughter who'd killed her mother in being born were a sign of the Fathers' anger. He showed us the bitterness he could not show toward the Fathers.

"Fortunately, he died when Miera and I were young enough for my grandfather to heal some of the wounds. My grandfather thinks his son's death was bad luck, but I do not. When I come to rule Nainan, I will be very young, but I will be a better Duke than I would have been if I'd endured my father for another twenty years."

They dismounted where their previous fencing bouts had already worn the grass away and packed the earth hard. They went through their warming-up exercises, then pulled on mail coats and the special fencing helmets with visors. Blade didn't expect these new helmets to become popular for war in a Dimension without archery. All he wanted was to keep himself or Chenosh from accidentally losing an eye.

They spent an hour doing exercises, then rested and talked. After that they fought three free-style matches. As usual Blade won all three, but his margin of victory was shrinking steadily.

"You're going to score your first victory before long," he told Chenosh when they were wiping off the sweat afterward. "My longer reach already does as much for me as my skill."

Chenosh frowned. "You mean that?"

"I haven't any reason to flatter you, Chenosh. So don't bristle as if I was one of your grandfather's courtiers. How long do you think I would live if you got yourself killed by believing my false praise? I value my own skin as much as any honorable Lord can do!"

Chenosh laughed. "Blade, I am beginning to believe that you are really as honest as you say you are." The pleasure left his face. "I wish—I wish my father had been like you, Blade. If he had been, both Miera and I . . ."

Blade found himself unable to look an eighteen-year-old boy in the face. It struck him that if he'd led a more normal life in Home Dimension, he might by now very well have a son not much younger than Chenosh. He'd fathered children in a good many Dimensions and even knew the fate of one of them—Rikard, who might still be ruling the land called Tharn. None of this was quite the same as being able to raise, teach, and send out into the world a child of his own.

"Well," he said. "The Fathers send each of us where they will. The only thing we can do is the best we can wherever they send us. You've certainly lived your life that way, and I've tried to do the same. Perhaps that's what draws us together."

"Perhaps," said Chenosh. Then, seeing Blade's embarrassment, he changed the subject. If he was going to fight without a shield or with only a small one, what about special armor for his right arm? A piece of heavy plate extending from the elbow down to the wrist would make it harder for an opponent to draw blood. It would also balance the sword in his left hand, and perhaps even let him use his right arm as a weapon. The arm itself was sound enough; it was only the hand which was crippled.

By the time they'd mounted their horses and were riding back to Castle Ranit, Blade was so interested in this new subject that he'd forgotten the embarrassing moment in the field.

Then there were dinners with Miera.

Sometimes Chenosh joined his sister, sometimes there was only the girl herself with her nurse as chaperone.

It was after dinner one evening, and they were nibbling salted nuts and drinking beer. Wine was the more lordly drink, but Miera preferred beer. They talked of the day's news and events.

"What have you heard about the Captain of the Duke's Guard?" asked Miera.

"Only the same thing everyone's heard. He fell from his horse last night and smashed one leg so badly he may never walk right again."

"Have you heard that he was drunk?"

66

"Are you telling me or asking me?" replied Blade, with a grin. He enjoyed these verbal games with Miera, even though he knew they were considered highly improper for an unmarried woman. However, Miera didn't care a fig for propriety, and for once her grandfather and Marshal Alsin seemed willing to let her have her own way.

"Asking," she said. "By all the stories I've heard he was a fine rider, too good to fall unless he was drunk."

"I haven't heard that he was drunk, either," said Blade cautiously. He was aware of the nurse at the other end of the table, well within hearing. He was also aware of his desire to go on treating Miera like a human being, instead of the way the Lords of this land were expected to treat even the best-born women. "It was raining a little," he added. "The road might have been wet, and he was riding fast the way he always did."

"Yes. It might have been wet." A man would have to be deaf not to hear the skepticism in Miera's voice. Then she smiled, her familiar mixture of innocence and sensuality. "I will not press you to tell me what you could not even if you knew it. You have already told me more than anyone except my brother would tell a woman." She reached a hand across the table and rested two fingers lightly on Blade's wrist. Then she jerked the hand back, as they both heard the nurse hissing like an indignant snake.

Finally, there was getting a Feathered One of his own.

Blade wasn't sure he needed or wanted one, but he seemed to be the only person who thought that. Everyone else assumed that a Lord of his qualities would want his own Feathered One. Even Miera joined her voice to the chorus, one of the few times he'd heard her agree with her grandfather and Alsin in public.

So finally Blade rode off to the ancient castle where the Duchy's Feathered Ones were bred and trained. The castle was the original seat of the Dukes of Nainan, turned over to the Masters of the Feathers when Castle Ranit was finished a century ago.

Since the Duke hadn't appointed a new Master to replace Orric, the place was in charge of Romiss, the Breeder. Romiss was not a Lord by rank, but unlike other non-Lords Blade had met in Nainan, he paid a Lord no unnecessary deference or servility. He knew he was a master of a skilled and demanding craft, and in the matter of choosing Feathered Ones he considered himself the equal of any Lord or even the Duke himself.

"This place is not what it was," said Romiss at once. "I'll say nothing against you for killing Orric. That was Lords' business. But the Duke's going to have to put someone in his place. I'll thank you to say as much the next time you have his ear."

"Orric knew his job, I understand." Blade wanted to draw Romiss into talking about his late master. He wasn't the sort to talk freely, and so far the Duke saw no reason to have him imprisoned and tortured. But if he accidentally dropped a hint here and there . . .

Romiss did most of the talking as the two men toured the castle. Each Feathered One had a little open wooden cage hung on the wall of a room in the castle. Each room had food, water, and sanitary facilities for its twenty or thirty Feathered Ones. There was also a hospital with a trained veterinarian for sick or pregnant monkeys, a nursery for the young ones, and even a cemetery out in the courtyard for those who died in the castle. Feathered Ones who died in the service of Lords were usually granted elaborately decorated little tombs.

With all the lecturing Romiss did, Blade didn't learn much about his late Master Orric, and nothing about the legend of the Feathered Ones and the meteorite. More immediately important, he didn't learn a thing about how to chose his own Feathered One. Should he go "eeeny-meeny-miny-mo," look at pedigree, take one home on a trial basis, or simply wait until that mysterious "telepathic link" established itself—if it ever did.

They were climbing the stairs from the hospital when they heard a sudden *yip-yip-yip* from the head of the stairs. The door flew open and a bucket, several brooms, and four Feathered Ones came crashing, rattling, and squeaking down the stairs. Romiss let out an oath and Blade got ready to fend the little beasts off with the flat of his sword. Sometimes they got out of their rooms and into the wine, then they could be hard to handle.

One of the Feathered Ones was noticeably larger than the other three, but had the most ragged feathers Blade had ever seen. As the monkeys reached the foot of the stairs, the other three turned on the large one. He promptly kicked one opponent in the face, pulled a handful of feathers out of a second one's head, then dashed back up the stairs. His opponents followed. With a tremendous leap the big monkey hurled himself into the air and landed on the highest spot in sight: Richard Blade's shoulder.

Romiss swore again. "That's Raggedy, the little—! He's never found a master, and for some reason he doesn't get along with his mates. They'd have killed him a long time ago if it wasn't for his being so good at escaping. Usually he gets out alone, but this time the other three must have been expecting something like that. So they followed him."

Romiss seemed to be casually assuming a rather high degree of intelligence in the Feathered Ones. Blade decided to play along with him. "Do you think the word about Raggedy is getting around?"

Romiss scratched his shaggy gray head. "Hope not," he said after a moment. "Then he won't last long. Kinder to take him out and kill him now."

At those words Raggedy's feathers bristled as much as they could, his eyes narrowed to slits, and his mouth opened to display all his yellow teeth. It looked to Blade very much as if he'd understood the words!

"Does he have any other vices besides escaping?" he asked.

Romiss shook his head. "Not that I know of, although it'll be awhile before he makes any sort of a show, with his feathers—You aren't going to *take* him, are you?"

"Why not?"

"The Duke wouldn't like you being given a Feathered One who couldn't—"

"Why don't we let the Duke speak for himself, my friend? He told me only to come and find a Feathered One who suited me. I think this one will suit me." Unspoken was Blade's thought: *He's lived alone, too. We should understand each other.*

Romiss swallowed, looked at Blade, then at Raggedy,

69

then shrugged. "He's yours, then. You'll be paying, of course, and the papers—"

"The Duke will be taking care of all that," said Blade, absentmindedly scratching the Feathered One's head. The monkey resented the liberty, and showed it by nipping Blade's left ear.

"Ouch! Cheeky little bugger, aren't you? In fact I think that's going to be your new name. From now on you're Cheeky."

"That's not a lordly name, Lord Blade. I hate to remind you of something like this, but—"

"Then don't remind me of it, Romiss. 'Cheeky' is the name he's been given by a Lord. Therefore it's a lordly name."

Romiss swallowed harder, realizing he'd gone further than even a Lord as tolerant as Blade would probably allow. "My apologies, Lord Blade."

"Accepted," said Blade, and it seemed to him that even if Romiss was somewhat withdrawn, he was at least a decent man, unlikely to have anything to do with any of Orric's treachery. Blade sheathed his sword and strode up the stairs, with Cheeky clinging to his hair. As they reached the top of the stairs, Cheeky squealed in delight, then turned his rump to his late comrades and waved his tale in derisive farewell.

Chapter 11

It was longer than Blade expected before Duke Cyron called him to a private meeting to hear the story of how he came to be an exile and a wanderer. Blade had plenty of time to prepare his "cover" story. He used all his experience in intelligence work, and drew freely on several Home Dimension medieval romances, a couple of historical novels, and some of the more romantic episodes of English history. The result might have made a fairly good novel in itself. Blade made mental note to write it down, in case he was seized with a desire to take up writing historical novels if he lived to retire! Certainly the story seemed to convince Duke Cyron that he was not only a Lord but a man who could be trusted. Three days after the meeting, he was invited to a private dinner in the Duke's chambers, with Alsin, Chenosh, and Miera, as well as Cyron himself.

"You've seen how much our Lords are willing to spend on their pleasures, haven't you?" said Alsin. He was sipping wine as he spoke, but Blade knew the question was more than casual. He'd seen another of those looks passing between Alsin and Duke Cyron over the candied fruits. Then the servants left one by one, until the lordly guests were alone and Alsin himself was pouring the wine.

Blade nodded. "I've seen the spending, at least. I won't judge the pleasures. Most of them aren't what I would care for, but I've lived a very different kind of life for many years. I've had less time for pleasures of any sort than the Lords of the Crimson River."

Another look passed between the Marshal and the Duke. Blade wondered if *they* had a telepathic link. So far he hadn't found one with Cheeky, but he and the feather-monkey seemed to understand each other well enough without it.

Duke Cyron sighed. "Do you think perhaps, Blade, the Lords' pleasures are excessive and that harm will come to the Duchies? I cannot command you to speak plainly, but I will be much happier if you do."

Now we're getting close to the heart of things, thought Blade. Aloud, he said, "If the Duchies have no enemies, they can afford to waste lives and wealth this way. It's not good, but nothing really bad will come of it. The question is: do the Duchies have enemies? I imagine they do."

"You judge correctly. I expected you would, and I thank the Fathers I was not disappointed." The emotion in the Duke's voice was so strong that both Alsin and Chenosh looked embarrassed. Blade felt a twinge of guilt. The Duke was clearly about to reveal his most cherished secrets to a man who'd won his confidence by an elaborate set of lies.

Once the Duke started explaining things his voice was clear, steady, and strong. For a while Blade was able to see him as he must have been at Blade's age—a strong, proud, and wise leader of men. The pride was still there and so was the wisdom, but now he had to do most of his work with the strength of younger men.

The seven Duchies of the Crimson River won their independence when both the East and West Kingdoms had civil wars within a generation. All seven Dukes fought side by side against the Kingdoms, then went their separate ways as soon as the fighting was over.

The two Kingdoms did just the opposite. Generation after generation, the Kings hammered their Lords into obedience, if not always into loyalty. For the last fifty years the two Kingdoms had been united and peaceful. Their wealth increased rapidly, and so did their armies.

Meanwhile, the seven Duchies and their Lords slid further and further into petty warfare and expensive vices. Every year they wasted enough wealth to raise an army, as completely as if they'd thrown the gold straight into the Crimson River.

"The warfare does give us some advantages," said Alsin. "Our Lords are better fighters, tougher, stronger, more experienced than most servants of the Kings. But our warfare also kills too many Lords and divides the rest so they will not willingly fight side by side. Either Kingdom can put into the field twice our strength in mounted Lords, to say nothing of Helpers. It is said that King Handryg of the West is even arming peasants!"

Duke Cyron shook his head. "I have heard this vile rumor, but I refuse to believe it is anything more. King Handryg has much that is unlordly about him, but he is not a fool or a barbarian."

Blade couldn't help feeling that anyone in this Dimension who *didn't* see that arming the peasants would give him an enormous advantage was an even bigger fool. He also knew that he'd be thrown out of Castle Ranit, possibly without his head, if he breathed a word of that thought.

72

Either Kingdom could have conquered the Crimson River lands twenty years ago, if they'd been ready to pay a high price. The Lords would sell their lives dearly, and the two Dukes whose Duchies controlled the passes to the Kingdoms were both honest and intelligent men. One of them, Duke Pirod of Skandra, was probably the best military mind along the Crimson River. The other, Duke Ormess of Hauga, had one of the strongest armies in the lands.

However, the time might come when the price for conquering the Crimson River would drop sharply. It would certainly come sooner if the Duchies remained divided and the Lords went on with their private quarrels and vices.

Then one of the Kingdoms would surely strike. King Fedron of the East was young, tough, a formidable soldier, and ruthlessly ambitious. King Handryg of the West was older, but he had the larger army. He might want to end his long reign with the glorious achievement of conquering the Duchies.

Either way, the Crimson River lands would suffer. The Dukes and Lords would fight for their honor even if they had no hope of victory. They would keep the war going until they were killed and their lands ruined. Duke Cyron painted a nightmarish picture of Alsin reduced to a mercenary in some foreign Lord's service, his grandson Chenosh a clerk or priest, and Miera forcibly married to some King's lowborn minister.

Blade couldn't help noting that neither Cyron nor Alsin said a word about the fate of the Crimson River's peasants during these years of warfare. They would have to worry about murder, starvation, torture, and rape, not just loss of rank, wealth, or honor.

Again, there was nothing to be gained by raising the point.

Besides, if the Duke had a plan for preventing the war, he'd be saving the peasants in spite of thinking only about the Lords. Blade began to wish the Duke would finish the "background briefing" and get on to the plan.

He didn't have to wait long. "Conquering the Duchies will still cost the Kingdoms too much if we all stand together," said Cyron. "It has been my hope for many years to find a way to unite the Duchies. Now I think the coming of Lord Blade gives us that way."

"You rest many hopes on me, Your Grace. I hope not too many." Blade wasn't being falsely modest. He honestly didn't know what was expected of him.

"You have traveled far, seen much, and thought deeply," said the Duke. "You bring to the Crimson River knowledge gained elsewhere. And you do not come from either Kingdom. All this makes you unlike any Lord I have known these past fifty years. Even if you are not good enough, Blade, I will not live long enough to wait for someone who might not be better and indeed might not come at all! I must do the best I can with your help. If that is not good enough—well, the Fathers do no honor to those who sit like frogs waiting for the snake to strike."

Cyron knew he had two of his fellow Dukes on his side, the two who held the passes. That meant four Dukes to win over or defeat. From what he knew of them they'd be hard to win over in the time available. On the other hand, all four of them had weaknesses which might be turned against them. The skills of all the men in the room now would be needed for this, but if they all worked together . . . Blade found himself wanting to hear more than tantalizing hints about the "weaknesses" of the other four Dukes, but didn't expect Cyron to tell him until he'd sworn to aid the Duke's plans.

Once all seven Duchies were willing to follow Cyron's leadership, they would be a match for either Kingdom. Then they could negotiate with the Kingdoms as equals, promising their allegiance to whichever King offered the better price. The Duchies would lose some of their independence, but they could hardly hope to keep that anyway. Instead they would gain a favored position under their new King, and they would be spared a destructive war.

Blade had one more question. He thought he knew the answer already, but he wanted to hear what Cyron and Alsin had to say. "If the Duchies end up willing to follow Your Grace, what is there to keep you from making them a third Kingdom, with yourself as King?"

"If I were twenty years younger or if my son were alive—nothing. As it is"—Cyron shrugged, and for the first time that evening he really looked his age—"I am past eighty. My lawful heirs are a grandson unseasoned in war and a granddaughter. Miera cannot inherit a crown at all, and Chenosh could not do so without much dispute. There would surely be enough warfare over the succession to undo all my work."

He looked sharply at Blade. "I have also thought of adopting an heir. But there are already men nearer to me in blood than you. Even they would not be sure of an undisputed succession. So that custom of the old days offers us no help."

"I had no ambitions to be adopted as your heir," said Blade in a level voice, and he decided to take a gamble. "If you had not done this for your bastard son Marshal Alsin, you would surely not do it for an outland Lord."

Cyron blinked. "You speak rather sharply for one who is, as you say, outlander."

"I think I speak the truth, too." Blade was sure now that the physical resemblance between Alsin and Cyron was no mere coincidence, and he was also sure that by speaking bluntly about their relationship he had done the right thing. Cyron now had to either make him an ally or kill him, and no man would kill a potentially useful ally merely for plain speaking. Besides, Blade was getting tired of all this verbal fencing. It was time to get to work.

"Yes. Alsin is my illegitmate son. So he could neither become my heir, nor do what *you* can do."

"And what is that?"

"Marry Miera, and become Captain of my Guards. That will bind you to me in blood and battle oath, so that you can act and speak for me. When you have done these things, we can set about the work you seem so impatient to begin."

Blade smiled in spite of himself. Cyron might be near-sighted, but when it came to seeing what made other people tick he missed very little. Blade poured himself more wine, conscious that Miera's eyes were on him all the while, then drank half the cup before speaking.

"As to marrying Miera"—he turned to face her—"my lady, it is for you to say whether you will have me as a husband or not. Is it *your* wish?"

"Blade, if you—" began Alsin irritably, but the Duke waved him to silence, and Chenosh glared at him. Miera was clutching the tablecloth in one hand and her knife in the other, so tightly her knuckles were white. Gently Blade reached over and pulled the knife out of her hand.

"Yes, my lord," she said finally, so quietly that Blade had to strain to hear her. "Yes, yes, yes, yes." For a moment it looked as if she were going to faint. Then her hand leaped out and clutched Blade's, and her smile seemed to light up the whole room. For a moment Blade had eyes for nothing else except that smile.

Cyron's almost apologetic cough brought him back to reality. "What about the Captaincy of my Guards?"

"I'll answer that when you've answered a question of mine," said Blade. This would be the bluntest question yet, but also the least dangerous. He'd gone too far for the Duke to turn against him now. "What happened to my predecessor? Did he really fall from his horse? And if he did, was it an accident?"

Chenosh answered, in spite of yet another sharp look from Alsin. "Lord Blade, I swear by the Fathers and my friendship for you that he whose place you take did fall, and by accident." Then he smiled. "I will *not* swear that the accident wasn't a piece of good luck for us, though."

The Duke nodded. "I add my word to his. Would we have set aside a faithful or at least useful servant before we could even be sure you would join us?"

"Wise men would not, that is true. But I did not know how faithful he was. Also, I have seen many strange things done in plots and conspiracies."

Alsin snorted. "You've seen nothing, compared to what you'll be seeing here."

Blade looked around the table and decided this was probably true. Then he looked at Miera again. Her green eyes were full of tears, but met his steadily. At least there was *one* person in this room he could trust!

Chapter 12

Blade was bethrothed to Miera three days after the dinner party, and married to her a week after that. She didn't object to the haste. In fact, she was so clearly *not* objecting that Alsin said she didn't have a lordly maiden's proper modesty.

At this, Chenosh finally lost his temper with the Marshal. "What is it, Alsin, that makes you so foolish about little things and so wise about big ones? Do you think people will forget you are a bastard if you guard the virtue of every woman around you, whether she wants to be guarded or not? You did not think to guard my sister from Orric's suit. Indeed, I always thought that you somewhat favored it—"

"That's a lie!" bellowed Alsin, in a voice which brought guards running to see who was killing whom. "I never favored Orric's suit. I only favored Miera's being wed, at a time when Orric was the only man who—"

"Do you mean to say my sister Miera is an undesirable match? If that is so, then you have spoken—"

Before Chenosh could finish the ritual phrase which would threaten a duel between him and Alsin, Blade stepped between the two men. "If I hear another word out of either of you, I'll have to tell the Duke," he snapped. He looked at the guards standing around, trying not to listen or at least to look as if they weren't listening. "I may have to tell the Duke anyway, or these men will spread tales. Chenosh, I think you owe Alsin an apology for questioning his judgment. Alsin, I think you owe me an apology for questioning the character of your Duke's kin and my intended bride."

Both men sighed, both apologized, and Alsin tramped off, back and shoulders stiff with indignation. Chenosh stayed behind, apparently wanting to speak with Blade, but it was Blade who spoke first.

"I hadn't heard that Orric offered for Miera's hand," he said in a level voice. "I think it is something I ought to have known. Did someone forget to tell me, or——?"

"No. No one forgot to tell you," said Chenosh hastily. He blushed red so that Blade found it hard to doubt his honesty. "Orric never made a proper offer. It was just that for some months he acted as if Miera would have to accept his offer when he made one. Alsin never did anything to support Orric except remind my father not to ignore him entirely until his disloyalty was a proven thing."

"I see. I hope you'll remember that the next time you lose your temper with the Marshal." Blade turned away, believing Chenosh but not wanting to talk with him anymore right now. An unpleasant question pricked at his mind. *Is Miera happy to marry me only because I saved her from Orric?*

There was some vanity in that question, but most of it was concern for Miera. The girl would be a widow before long, whether Blade was killed in battle or survived to return to Home Dimension. Inevitably she would have to remarry. Then she would have all the pain of learning the ways of a Crimson River husband after getting used to Blade. She might be better off marrying one of her own people, and letting her grandfather join Blade to his house with some other female relative.

Unfortunately the ducal house of Nainan was dying out, so there might not be any other woman for Blade to marry. Even if there were, it was probably too late to raise the question without offending the Duke. Then Miera would suffer her grandfather's anger, instead of having at least a few months of as much happiness as Blade could give her.

He still couldn't help wondering whether Miera would look up at him from the bridal bed with reluctance, or even fear. He also wondered how many more family secrets the leaders of the Duchy were hiding from him. Was he an ally or a tool? And did they know the answer to that question themselves?

The day of the wedding dawned bright, promising heat later. Blade was glad they would be holding the ceremony in the coolness of the morning. His wedding robe was stiff with embroidery and jewels and lined with fur, while Miera's wedding gown must have weighed as much as a suit of armor.

It was a small wedding, for a ducal house. Cyron had delayed the ceremony just long enough to let all the people who *had* to be witnesses ride in from their castles. Including the armed Guardsmen, no more than forty people rode out of Castle Ranit to the Sacred Grove downstream. There the Dukes of Nainan had taken their brides, acknowledged their heirs, received the allegiance of their Lords, and lain on their funeral pyres for centuries.

The Guardsmen took up their positions around the grove. They were all armed to the teeth, and Alsin would see that they stayed alert. With so little warning, it wasn't likely that any of the Duke's enemies could have prepared a major attack to break up the wedding. A handful of skilled assassins riding fast was another matter.

In the center of the grove was an open space with a stone altar and a metal reflector for the ceremonial fire behind it. Everyone except Blade and Miera dropped back as the priest led the way toward the altar. He held the ceremonial torch high, and brandished it as if it were a sword. He probably wished it were. Like most of the priests of the Fathers, this man was a Lord, either too old to fight or else forced into the priesthood by enemies.

The priest began pouring the grain, wine, spices, and butter over the sticks piled on the altar. With half his mind Blade watched the ritual. He wondered how many times he was now a bigamist, in how many different Dimensions? He hadn't lost count of the women, but he couldn't remember all the marriage laws and customs. Certainly no bigamist was ever as sure as Richard Blade that his various "wives" wouldn't learn about one another!

The rest of his attention was on Miera, trying to read the small masklike face shadowed by the great embroidered

79

hood. Her eyes were aimed firmly at the ground, her mouth was steady, and it was too dark in the grove to see if she was pale under her heavy makeup.

The priest finished preparing the ceremonial fire, then called on the watchers to bear witness as he dropped the torch onto the sticks. They had been soaked in resin so they would burn even after being drenched with wine, and the flames roared up with an impressive crackling. Blade had to brush embers off Miera's hood.

Then the fire showed him something which drove Miera right out of his mind. The flames lit up the reflector behind the altar. Blade saw the side toward the fire was machine smooth under its coating of ancient soot. The edges were curled and curved as if they'd been cut with a torch or perhaps torn by an explosion. In the center of the reflector was a circular disk, with a hole on either side and three unmistakable bolts holding it in place. Blade wished he dared to move far enough to see the other side of the reflector. From where he was it remained tantalizingly beyond his field of vision.

That reflector was a piece of worked metal, far beyond any technology he'd seen or heard of in this Dimension. Where did it come from? Blade thought of the legend of the "falling star" and the Feathered Ones. Was the reflector a piece of a spaceship which brought the feather-monkeys to this world? Did the priest know enough about its origins to make it worthwhile asking him any questions?

Blade realized suddenly that the priest was looking at him impatiently. The actual oath taking by the bridal couple must be about to start. Blade remembered that a single misspoken or omitted word could make the marriage invalid, and forced himself to concentrate on the oaths he'd memorized so carefully.

Yet he couldn't get the mystery of the reflector out of his mind, until the time came to kiss the bride. He gripped Miera's hood with both hands and pushed it back from her face. The hood was so stiff with embroidery that it was like raising a rusty visor on a helmet. Then he saw that her eyes were almost closed, and tears were making trails down both cheeks.

This will never do, he thought. Miera must have seen

that his thoughts were elsewhere and come to the conclusion that he was reluctant to marry *her*! He bent and kissed her much harder than custom required. Her lips didn't quite open under his, but after a moment they started trembling. Then he heard the shouts of the witnesses as they all hailed the newlyweds, and the priest raising his voice in a triumphant chant.

Duke Cyron came forward and led Blade and Miera away from the altar. Blade wanted to look back for a final glimpse of the mysterious reflector, but the memory of the tears on Miera's face made him keep looking at her.

Outside the narrow window of the bridal chamber, rain was falling. Its sound drowned out Blade's footsteps as he pulled the door shut behind him and walked across the carpeted stone floor toward the bed. The chamber was dark except for one small candle perched on a low table beside the window. In the light of that candle, he thought he saw something move outside the window. A second look showed nothing.

Probably just candlelight reflected on the rain.

He walked to the huge canopied bed, pulled open the curtains, and peered inside. He'd expected to find Miera already snuggled down under the blankets, and half hoped to find her asleep. If she was, they could consummate the marriage in the morning just as well as tonight, and never mind the people outside waiting for the groom's announcement! At least this wasn't one of those Dimensions where the witnesses stood around the bed itself, listening for the bride's cry!

The bed was empty. Blade shut the curtains, turned, and searched the room with his eyes. At first it seemed that Miera had vanished entirely. He had a momentary nasty thought of secret passages. Then he saw a patch of paler darkness in one corner. He walked over and pulled the hood of Miera's night robe back from her head. She smiled stiffly up at him as he undid the brooch which held the robe at her throat. The robe dropped to the floor, leaving Miera standing only in a green silk shift with lace at the wrists and throat. It was just thin enough to give Blade tantalizing hints of the lovely body inside.

81

"Get yourself into bed, Miera," he said softly. "You'll be cold standing here." She shook her head and didn't move, except to flinch when he laid a hand on her shoulder to steer her toward the bed. He gave up and started pulling his own bed robe over his head.

He'd completely covered his head when he heard Miera scream. At the same time something landed hard on top of the robe. Blade's first thought was, *Assassins*! Then he heard a familiar *yip-yip-yip*.

Cheeky!

Blade jerked the robe down so violently that seams ripped. Cheeky held on, until Blade wanted to yell at the pain of having his hair pulled out in monkey-sized handfuls. Then the Feathered One bent far forward, holding on with both feet and looping his tail around his master's neck. Both hands clutched at the shoulder of Miera's shift, sharp little claws pierced the fabric, and there was a brisk ripping sound. The shift gaped and started to slide off Miera's body, she screamed again, and Blade let out a roar of fury.

Everyone in the hall must have heard that roar. Fists started hammering on the locked door, and Blade heard his name called. He reached up, gripped Cheeky firmly with both hands, and pulled him free. Blade was half-choked before the feather-monkey unwound his tail, and several more clumps of hair came free.

He held Cheeky out in front of him at arm's length. For a long moment he understood why some Lords murdered their Feathered Ones. He looked at Miera, cowering in a corner and clutching her shift to her body, and fought a strong urge to hurl Cheeky out the window. The little brute must have climbed up the outside wall of the keep as soon as he knew which room Blade would be using!

As he glared at Cheeky, a change came over the feather-monkey. His eyes closed, his tail curled up tightly, and he gave a little whimper. He knew he'd gone much too far, that Blade wasn't taking his prank as a joke. He was very sorry. One hand reached out toward Miera. She stiffened, then forced herself to take a step forward. Cheeky patted her on the forehead and whimpered again.

Then with a splintering crash the locked door flew open,

broken down from the outside. Half a dozen of the would-be witnesses sprawled in a pile on the rug. Miera jumped, lost her grip on her shift, and for a moment stood stark naked in front of the men on the floor. Blade moved to get in front of her, but she darted across the room and vanished through the curtains of the bed. He swore again under his breath, then sighed. He hoped the rest of this marriage would be better than the wedding night, which was beginning to look like a complete disaster.

The men on the floor untangled themselves and stood up, apologizing for having let their fears for his and Miera's safety get the better of them. He listened to the apologies in a chilly silence, then held out Cheeky.

"Take my little friend here and see that he stays out of this room. Give him some wine, and maybe he'll go to sleep." He scratched Cheeky's back, and the feather-monkey squirmed with pleasure. "You'll never know how close you came to being splattered all over the wall, you little bastard!"

When the door closed again, Blade promptly dragged every loose piece of furniture in the room in front of the door. Nobody else was going to get in tonight without using a battering ram! He was stripping off his bed robe again when a thought struck him. The way Cheeky had behaved when he realized he'd gone too far had indeed seemed to indicate that the Feathered One was apologizing. But why had Blade actually heard the words "I'm sorry" in his head?

He stood naked in the middle of the room, ignoring the chilly breeze from the window on his bare skin as he considered what had happened. He didn't doubt the existence of telepathy and perhaps other paranormal forces. He'd experienced telepathy himself. So he wasn't going to dismiss the possibility that the Feathered Ones really were telepathic. But this was the first time he had received anything he could recognize as a message from Cheeky. Perhaps in the past the Feathered One's telepathy was too subtle. Or perhaps Blade had just made a lucky guess about that Cheeky wanted to tell him this time. He wished he'd been able to learn more from Breeder Romiss about the Feathered Ones, or else have watched them in action more. . . .

A faint sound from the bed broke into his thoughts. He listened, and it came again. It sounded like a stifled giggle, and he was relieved. At least he hadn't made Miera cry again, by thinking about the Feathered Ones' telepathy when he should have been thinking of her. If he'd done that, he wouldn't have easily forgiven himself.

It was time to go to bed. The bride was getting impatient.

Blade tiptoed across the rug to the bed, then suddenly jerked the curtains aside. Miera was lying naked on top of the blankets, her face buried in one of the pillows, shaking with laughter. She looked up and gave a squeak of surprise, as he patted her on the rump. Her buttocks were nicely turned, firm and warm, strongly tempting his hand to linger. He pulled it back—better not rush things.

"I hope that trouble with the Feathered One didn't bother you too much," he said. "If you'd like me to get rid of Cheeky—"

"Oh, no. You mustn't promise too much on our wedding night. Don't you know that's the one night of his life when a Lord's promises to a woman are sacred? If you promise to send Cheeky away tonight, you'll have to do it. I don't think he would like that. I've seen him when you weren't looking, and he is yours for life if you'll let him stay."

"Whose life?" said Blade with a laugh. "His or mine? *His* life won't be very long if he frightens you again."

Miera sat up, still naked but with her hands covering her breasts, and her legs together. "He didn't really frighten me, Richard. I was angry more than frightened, but I think you better try some more discipline—" She mimed turning Cheeky over her knee and spanking him like a baby.

Blade stared. To make this gesture, Miera had to expose her breasts, and they were simply breathtaking. They were perfect cones without the slightest sag, and a creamy white except for a light dusting of freckles and the pink nipples, which were neither too large nor too small. . . .

His hands reached out to cup her breasts as if his fingers had a will of their own. Miera gave a little gasp as she felt a man's flesh against hers for the first time in her life.

Then she bent forward, so that her breasts pressed harder into his hands. She reached out with both hands and gripped his shoulders, pulling him toward her as her mouth opened. Blade didn't know if she wanted to say something or to be kissed. He didn't let her speak, because he couldn't have held back from kissing her if there'd been a gun pointed at his head.

Her lips stayed open as they met his. After a little while her tongue also crept out to meet his. Its movements were fumbling, like the movements of her hands. They were also determined. Miera wanted to do her best, even if she wasn't quite sure what that "best" ought to be.

Blade was relieved he wouldn't have to spend hours overcoming her fears. Before long his kisses moved from her lips, down her throat, and onto her breasts. They stayed there for quite a while, as his hands twined themselves in her silky, perfumed hair. At the same time her hands were running up and down over the muscles of his chest, probing the scars, sometimes making little darts down toward his groin. She always drew back before she touched his manhood, as if she were still afraid of being *too* bold.

It didn't matter. Blade was ready to take her long before he dared think she was ready for him. With a woman like Miera in his arms, a eunuch would have been aroused! He listened to sighs and whimpers of pleasure and watched her tossing her head from side to side for quite a while before he gently rolled her over on her back. Even then he stroked her thighs and belly and the damp red hair between her legs still longer before he raised himself above her.

She cried out at the moment of entry, but at the same time clutched him to her as if he was her only hope of life. *Oh, well, at least those bastards outside won't be able to say a thing against her virginity!* Then Blade set to work to give Miera as much pleasure as he could before his own control ran out.

She was moaning happily by the time that happened. He wasn't sure whether she'd found her own release or not, only knew that afterward she snuggled comfortably against him, as contented as a cream-filled kitten. At last he forced himself to get up and bring warm water to wash her thighs. By then she was awake again.

As he finished washing her, she pointed at his penis. "Shouldn't you wash too? After all . . ." She was too flustered to continue, and instead picked up the bowl and cloth and started washing his groin. Under the warm water and the warmer fingers, he felt himself stiffening again.

"Oh, my," she said, contemplating her work. "Oh, my." Then she bent over and kissed the tip of Blade's penis. Her lips trembled against his flesh for a moment, as if she wanted to do more. Then she drew back, gripping his hands to pull him after her.

This time she gasped instead of crying out when he entered. This time also there was no doubt she'd found her own release. Her happy scream must have been heard all over the keep as she arched her body against her husband's. She was half-stunned and more than half-limp when he poured himself into her. By the time he could fold her in his arms, she was sound asleep.

The smile hadn't deceived Blade. The sensuality was there in Miera, all right. It just required a little care to bring it out into the open, for his pleasure and hers.

Chapter 13

Making Blade Captain of the Duke's Guardsmen went more smoothly than his wedding night. It helped that Cheeky was kept firmly out of the way until the oath-taking ceremony was finished. It also helped that most of the hundred Guardsmen were perfectly happy to serve under him. The previous captain was a tough, hard man, who knew how to fight but not how to make friends or win the hearts of his men. Most of them hoped he would live and recover from his wounds, but no one particularly missed him.

Blade also came recommended by Lord Gennar and Lord Ebass. Gennar had the reputation of a man who would be burned alive rather than tell a lie, and Lord Ebass was one of the toughest fighters in Nainan. Most Guardsmen were ready to think well of any man who came recommended by those two.

"Some will still have their doubts about an outlander," said Alsin. "But they will also doubt the wisdom of challenging the man who slew Orric. His Grace does not make Guardsmen out of fools."

"Good," said Blade. "Do you know if he's made Guardsmen out of any of Orric's friends who might carry a grudge against his killer?"

Alsin's forehead wrinkled in concentration. "There are none in the Guards bound to Orric by ties of blood, public oath, or battle comradeship," he said slowly. "As to those who may consider themselves bound in other ways—I cannot swear one way or the other."

"I won't expect you to," said Blade. "Just help me watch my back, though. We may find them where and when we don't expect it."

"My hand on that," said the Marshal, and they made the four-handed shake of sworn comrades. Alsin might have harsh manners, especially toward women, but he also had more than his share of common sense. A man like Duke Cyron would hardly have made him Marshal otherwise, bastard son or not.

The worst problem Blade had to face in leading the Guardsmen was his inexperience in using the lance from horseback. This was a specialized technique of fighting which he knew he could hardly expect to master in a few weeks. It was also considered the most honorable way of fighting among the Lords of the Crimson River, although a few wise heads would admit that it wasn't always the most useful in war.

Blade won over the Guardsmen with an exhausting demonstration of everything else he could do on a horse. He could use sword, mace, morningstar, and the Guards' short throwing spear. He also had an excellent seat on a horse, and several Lords failed to knock him out of the saddle with their lances. So the Guardsmen knew their new Captain wouldn't make a fool of himself on horseback, and that was enough.

Between winning over the Guardsmen and keeping Miera happy, Blade was a busy man for some days. The moment he was free, Duke Cyron summoned him to another private meeting. There the Englishman learned more about the weaknesses of the Dukes of the Crimson River than he'd ever expected to know.

"If I had to choose which Duke to strike first, I'd choose Duke Padro of Gualdar," said Blade, after listening to Cyron and Alsin.

"Why?" said the two Lords in unison. *If those two don't have a telepathic link, I'd like to know what they do have,* Blade said to himself. To the others he said, "He's the youngest. That makes him the most likely to accept another Duke's leadership. He's the poorest, which means he's the one who can least afford a long war. Finally, his big vice is gambling on duels of Feathered Ones. That's a vice we can easily exploit."

"It seems as if you already have a plan for Duke Padro," said Cyron. "Could you tell us a little more?"

"I have a plan," said Blade carefully, "but I have to be sure of a few more details before it will be worth discussing. If I can have—"

"What sort of details?" said Alsin sharply, before Cyron could silence him.

"If they don't work out, my plan won't be worth talking about. If they do, you'll know everything as soon as I know it myself." He looked at Alsin. "You can be sure I'm not going to lead you by the nose into this, the way you led me into the duel with Orric."

Alsin glared, but Duke Cyron chuckled. "Point to Lord Blade, I think. Now—you were about to ask for something, to complete your plan?"

"Yes. Two or three days' time. If I'm not successful by then, I don't think I will be. At least not in time to help you in dealing with Duke Padro."

"Very well, Lord Blade. You have those three days. I wish you good fortune."

Blade thanked the Duke and left. He went straight back to his room in the keep, hoping he hadn't promised what he couldn't hope to perform. A large part of his reputation with the Duke now depended on Cheeky. However, if he succeeded, he'd be offering the quickest and cheapest way of dealing with Duke Padro. That would save time, gold, and fighting men, all of which would probably be needed for dealing with the other three hostile Dukes.

It was too bad they couldn't call on the two friendly Dukes for aid now, but it couldn't be helped. The two Dukes holding the passes to the East and West Kingdoms would need all their strength to continue to do just that. Otherwise, either Kingdom could invade at will, before Duke Cyron could finish his work.

There was also the need for secrecy. The more people helping with Duke Cyron's plans, the more who would have to know of it. Blade remembered the old saying of the Russian anarchists of the nineteenth century: "When four men sit down to plan revolution, three are fools and one is a police spy." The Duke was certainly planning a revolution, even if it was from the top down. He didn't have to worry about a Czar's secret police, but he certainly had to worry about many other enemies. The late Lord Orric's friends would be only one kind of enemy, and probably not the most dangerous.

These sober thoughts carried Blade all the way back to his room. It looked empty. He knew that Miera was still down in the hall with her maids, embroidering a pennant for him, and Cheeky was probably hiding as usual. The feather-monkey could hide himself in places Blade would have sworn weren't big enough for a cockroach, let alone twenty pounds of muscle and feathers.

He poured himself some beer, then got out a plate of Cheeky's favorite candied fruit. Before he'd taken two swallows, the feather-monkey popped out from under the stand holding the chamber pot. He squealed in delight as he saw the fruit, sat down in front of the bowl, and started stuffing himself with both hands.

Blade watched him with wry affection. He was getting

quite fond of the little beast, in spite of his maddening pranks, and hoped his plan wouldn't involve too much danger for Cheeky—but knew he could only hope. There was no way of telling in advance what the feather-monkey would be facing.

One thing was certain—right now Cheeky looked too healthy for Blade's plan. He was still thin, but his plucked-out feathers were growing back. He no longer looked like the ragged misfit he'd been when Blade found him. They'd have to do something about that, and that would mean finding out once and for all about this telepathy business.

He sat down on the bed and beckoned. The feather-monkey came slowly, holding out the empty fruit bowl. "No. No more. We have to talk."

"*Yeeecckkk!*" Cheeky sounded disgusted.

Blade used Yoga techniques to slow his breathing and relax his muscles. Then he started forming a clear mental image: Cheeky plucked and ragged again. It took him several tries before he could not only form the image but hold it for more than a few seconds. In between tries he cursed the bad luck which made the Wizard of Rentoro die in returning from Dimension X with him. That man had forgotten more about the powers of the mind than everybody in Home Dimension put together had learned! If he'd been able to teach a fraction of it, Blade's reaching Cheeky mentally could have been child's play!

At last he had the picture in his mind as clearly as if he'd been seeing it with his eyes. Cheeky was now sitting in front of him, staring curiously. What sort of funny trick was his master up to now? Blade wanted to hold his breath, but knew that would make his concentration weaker instead of stronger. The silence in the room was almost deafening. He hoped Miera wouldn't walk in now. . . .

Cheeky gave a sharp squeal of pure rage, and jumped three feet into the air. Then he started racing around the room like a mad thing, practically bouncing off the walls. Suddenly into Blade's mind came an image just as clear as the plucked Cheeky—his own dead body, lying on its funeral pyre.

He knew now that telepathy was indeed possible between himself and Cheeky. He also knew just what the feather-monkey was telling him: "If you pluck my feathers, I'll see you dead somehow!"

Blade suspected he'd made a mistake in choosing his first image. He'd wanted something vivid, certain to catch Cheeky's attention if the Feathered One had any survival instincts at all. Had he overdone things a little? If he had, that was a mistake he'd have to correct right now!

Blade started changing the image in his mind. It took fewer tries than the first time before he had the right picture under control. Now he had a picture of a plucked Cheeky, wearing a gold chain and embroidered gloves, sitting in front of bowls holding all his favorite foods, with a silver dagger and a jewel-tipped spear resting on silk cushions beside him. After a minute of that image Cheeky stopped bouncing off the walls. Another minute and he stopped broadcasting the angry picture of a dead Blade. Instead the man got the distinct feeling he was being asked some sort of question.

"What do you want me to do, that's worth having my feathers plucked again?" At least that seemed a good guess about what Cheeky would be saying if he was speaking in any sort of human words. Blade suspected there were going to be a lot more of these "good guesses" before he established any sort of reliable communication with the animal. It might take days and it would certainly take many hours.

He changed the image again, this time showing Cheeky sitting quietly at the foot of the bed. Blade was able to form this image on the first try and hold it on the second. Was telepathy something which became easier once you'd made the initial breakthrough? He hoped so.

"Yip?" Cheeky's call had an unmistakable questioning note.

Blade repeated the image of Cheeky sitting. This time Cheeky sat, too. Blade took out parchment and pen and wrote a short note to Miera, telling her to stay out of their room until after dinner. He could only say that he was "on important business for the Duke" a servant who could read might easily get a glimpse of the message on its way to Miera.

When the messenger was gone, he turned back to the

Feathered One who was still sitting quietly. For the first time Blade began to feel almost triumphant. He'd reached Cheeky with telepathy, proving both its existence *and* his ability to use it!

He sobered quickly, however. He'd made a good beginning, but nothing more. He still had to find ways of sending and receiving telepathic messages without taking so much time and attention. If he tried to concentrate like this in the middle of a battle, he'd be making himself an easy victim.

Could Cheeky understand messages sent in words, or would he need images? And once they'd worked out a common language of some sort, would Cheeky be interested in his master's plan? That was the biggest question of all. If he said "No," Blade's whole victory in establishing telepathic contact would be only theoretically interesting. No doubt Lord Leighton would still be fascinated when he heard the story, but Duke Cyron needed practical results. Would he get any?

Blade knew it was much too soon to answer that question. Cheeky, he suspected, was going to be stubborn about putting his life on the line, no matter what the reward. He remembered the time he'd been assigned to persuade a certain industrial espionage expert to work for MI6A. That was one of the most frustrating jobs J had ever dumped on him!

Blade poured himself some more beer, then filled Cheeky's bowl, and handed it to him. They both drank, then settled down to their "talk."

Talking Cheeky into cooperation was literally a headache for Blade. By the time he and the Feathered One shook hands on their bargain, the man felt as if he had the worst hangover of his life. He lurched to his feet and went over to the window.

No wonder he was tired and hungry! It was well after dark, and he'd sat down with Cheeky just after noon! He summoned more servants, and sent them both for dinner and Miera.

Blade yawned and signaled to Cheeky, who jumped up on his shoulder. As he scratched the Feathered One's back, he could almost feel the waves of pleasure he radiated. Cheeky was definitely going to be a "him" from now on. The Feathered One had too much intelligence to be called "it."

How *did* the Feathered Ones get that intelligence? The old question repeated itself. This time he felt more confident of getting close to the answer. Romiss the Breeder knew more about the Feathered Ones than he'd told any Lord. Blade was sure of that.

Romiss would talk to him, though. Blade would start by demonstrating telepathic links with Cheeky. Even if Romiss wasn't impressed, his men would be. He'd have to talk with Blade, to keep them quiet. Besides, the Breeder might be curious himself.

If this wasn't enough, there was always gold. Right now he didn't have much more than his clothes, weapons, and furniture, but if his plans worked out, that would soon change. After Cheeky finished with whatever opponent Duke Padro sent him, Blade would have enough gold to buy any man's secrets.

Chapter 14

They invited Duke Padro of Gualdar to match his best Feathered One against the chosen champion of Nainan. He accepted, and appeared before Castle Ranit only a few days later. So did Duke Garon of Ney and Duke Raskod of Issos. Instead of one hostile Duke, Cyron found himself playing host to three at once.

"It's a breach of custom and manners for them to be here at all without warning or invitation," fumed Alsin. He looked angry enough to call up Nainan's fighting Lords and chase the uninvited guests home.

"So it is," said Duke Cyron calmly. "I won't forget it, either. But I won't have a word said to either Garon or Raskod now. They hardly have enough men to put us in any danger, as long as we are alert and they are outside the castle. Nor will they enter it. Show a little respect for my judgment in war, Alsin."

"Yes, Your Grace." The tough Marshal swallowed. "We may even get some good from this," the Duke added. "Knowing the other Dukes are watching could make Padro even bolder than usual. If Garon says the wrong word, Padro may throw all caution to the winds!"

Blade found that the prospect of trying his plan under the eyes of three hostile Dukes didn't make *him* feel bolder. Failure would now be twice as public, twice as embarrassing, and twice as likely to ruin Cyron's hopes. There was no turning back, either, when the duel was going to be tomorrow!

He mentally gritted his teeth, determined to let no doubts show on his face. He'd laid his plans as carefully as he could and worked out all the details with Cheeky. It wasn't his fault or the Feathered One's that the stakes were suddenly so much higher. Blade still wondered if he really might be losing the proper balance between caution and boldness? Even worse, was he losing it where other people besides himself might be the victims? He'd have to talk to J about this when he returned to Home Dimension.

Blade might have slept better that night if his window hadn't given him a view of the camps of all three visiting Dukes. He could see the torches of the sentries, the cooking fires, the lanterns hanging from the tent doors. He could also see more torches lighting the work of the men smoothing down the game field for the monkey duel tomorrow.

Miera knew that something was bothering her husband, and did her best to make him forget it. Unfortunately she wasn't yet quite experienced enough in bed to succeed. Blade was able to give her all she wanted, but he himself lay awake for quite a while afterward.

He was still out of bed before dawn, walking through the camps of the three Dukes to get a firsthand picture of the enemy. He didn't quite trust Duke Cyron and Marshal Alsin enough to take their word on anything he could check for himself. Even if he'd trusted them more, he'd have made the tour of the camps. The most accurate information from someone else still wasn't quite the same as what you saw and heard yourself.

Duke Padro of Gualdar was in his early twenties, slim, dark, mustached, and good-looking in a rather effeminate fashion. Blade wasn't surprised to see a number of painted and perfumed young men drifting around his camp. Most of them wore swords, but they also wore such extravagant outfits of lace and ruffles, embroidery and gilded buttons, that Blade doubted that they'd be much good in a fight. They'd be too worried about getting spots on their clothing.

Padro's fops shared their luxurious tent with a dozen gigantic men in steel and leather. They roamed the Duke's camp, hard eyes searching every passing face, and scarred brown hands never far from the hilts of swords or throwing spears. Duke Padro's Master of the Feathers had a similarly efficient staff, and the tent which housed his Feathered Ones was the largest in his camp. It was also the best guarded.

Duke Garon of Ney was supposed to be the best jouster of any Duke for the last three generations. He certainly looked it—chunky, hard-muscled, bowlegged, and obviously hard as iron in spite of the gray in his hair. His men were nothing remarkable, but his horses were the finest Blade had seen in this Dimension. Finest of all was his chestnut war charger, Kanglo. Unlike Cyron or Padro, Duke Garon had plenty of heirs—four sons, as a matter of fact. None of the four was on good terms with any of the others, and much of Garon's time was spent keeping the peace among them. Wisely enough, he hadn't brought any of them with him.

Duke Raskod of Issos also had heirs, two sons and a daughter. One of the sons was feeble-witted, and neither of them was with him at Castle Ranit. Instead he'd brought his famous harem, or at least part of it. Blade counted six good-looking young women taking the air outside a closely guarded tent. Duke Raskod himself was nowhere in sight, but this didn't surprise Blade. The Duke was known all over the Crimson River lands for his laziness. He wouldn't be up much before breakfast unless his camp caught fire.

The thought of breakfast made Blade aware that he'd worked up an appetite touring the camps. He mounted his horse and rode back to the castle. On the way he saw a man walking alone beside the road. From a distance he looked so much like Chenosh that he drew rein.

"Lord Chenosh! May I offer you—oh, sorry." The man wore a merchant's garb, covered with dust and patches. He also stooped slightly, and his mustached face was much darker than Chenosh's. Blade rode on.

Blade ate an immense breakfast, alone except for Chenosh, who came in as he was nearly finished. Chenosh was freshly bathed, impressively dressed, and generally looking more like a Duke's heir than Blade had ever seen him. At least he would have looked this role if he hadn't been so obviously nervous. He ate little, drank less, kept looking everywhere except at Blade, and nearly jumped out of his seat at every unexpected noise. Blade was glad to see that someone else in Castle Ranit was also on edge!

As Chenosh finished eating, the trumpets and drums sounded to summon everyone to the dueling field.

Duke Padro's numerous enemies all admitted that he had at least one skill. He was an expert with the Feathered Ones, so much so that he hardly needed a Master of the Feathers. It was Duke Padro of Gualdar himself who strode forward onto the dueling field, carrying Gualdar's chosen champion. His Master of the Feathers followed at a respectful distance.

Padro set down the silk-covered cage, removed the cover, and let out Gualdar's champion, Posass. Posass was smaller than Cheeky, but beautifully groomed, with a silk vest and a belt of gold links. He was sleek and almost fat compared to Cheeky, but he moved well. Blade could also pick out the scars under the elegant feathers. Posass hadn't become the champion of a demanding master by sitting in his cage.

Now Blade strode forward, Cheeky riding casually on his shoulder. When they reached the center of the field, the monkey jumped down.

Duke Padro pulled at his mustache and stared at him. *"That* is your champion?"

"Do you doubt the word of Duke Cyron of Nainan?" said Blade.

"No, I—" Padro's olive skin turned darker. "This isn't a joke?"

"No, it's a Feathered One," said Blade. Padro's confusion was understandable. Cheeky's feathers looked even worse than they had when Blade found him, and skilled makeup by Chenosh made him look not only half-starved but diseased. He sat quietly at his master's feet, listlessly picking at a bald spot just above one knee.

"As you wish," said Padro. "But if there is any joke today, it will not be one the men of Nainan will find amusing. I want to double the Duke's wager, and give odds of three to one."

Blade did quick mental arithmetic. The Duke's wager on a duel of champion Feathered Ones was two thousand gold marks. That was a respectable sum for even Duke Cyron to find, and it would cripple Padro. Four thousand marks would nearly cripple Cyron if Cheeky lost. To be sure, Padro could never pay twelve thousand if he lost. Cyron would own him body and soul. Still, the duel had suddenly become more dangerous for Nainan than Blade liked.

He was turning to look at Cyron when a harsh voice shouted from the other side of the field. "Three to one, with that to fight? What's wrong with Posass, Padro? Or is it something wrong with your heart?"

Blade recognized the voice, and wanted to cheer. It was Duke Garon of Ney, who openly despised Padro as unworthy of his rank. He couldn't have picked better words to drive his young rival into doing something stupid, or a better time to say them.

Padro's smooth, carefully manicured fingers writhed like snakes. They were itching for a sword, or perhaps Garon's throat. Then Padro took a deep breath. "Well, Lord Blade. Have you the power to agree? Eight to one it will be, if you'll raise the stake to six thousand marks."

Losing six thousand marks would hardly leave Duke Cyron with two brass coins to rub together. On the other hand, forty-eight thousand marks was more money than

though he never was. Soon Posass began to scream and jump up and down, frustrated at being unable to hurt his opponent.

Blade looked around the field. Duke Padro and Duke Garon were looking at the field, grinning broadly. The third Duke, Raskod, had finally made his appearance, accompanied by a bevy of beauties from his harem, who were standing on the sidelines, eagerly watching the fight. The men of Nainan who knew Blade's plan—Cyron, Alsin, and Chenosh—were keeping masklike faces.

Everybody else from Nainan was looking grimmer and grimmer as the minutes went by, and Cheeky went on disgracing the Duchy. They also started shooting black looks at Blade, who made sure his sword and dagger moved freely in their scabbards. If by some chance Cheeky should lose, he was going to face an embarrassing choice. He could do what was honorable, by his own standards as well as by those of the Crimson River, and stay to die for his mistake. Or he could think of the future of Project Dimension X, take to his heels, and carve a path through anyone who got in his way.

He sincerely hoped he wouldn't have to make this particular decision.

Certainly no one from the other three Duchies seemed to doubt how the fight would end. They screamed and shouted obscene taunts at Cheeky, making such a din that finally Duke Padro himself had to call for silence. After that they were content with making more side bets. They still talked loudly enough to let Blade hear some bets being made at odds of twelve and fifteen to one. A lot of purses might be empty by the end of the day. Blade hoped there would not also be a lot of desperate men, ready to attack Duke Cyron and Nainan. There could be such a thing as too big a victory!

The duel went on, still more of a chase than a real fight. Blade began to wish he could reach Cheeky mind to mind, but knew that would be impossible in this fight. Posass would catch up with his opponent in a moment if he slowed down to talk to Blade. Then Cheeky would be too busy defending himself to concentrate on a mental message. Besides, Posass or his master might "hear" the message. Then the important advantage their secret gave Blade and Cheeky would be gone for good.

Around and around the Feathered Ones went. The fancy clothing of Duke Padro's courtiers was beginning to look the worse for the heat and the dust. The ladies of Duke Raskod's harem even took off some of their clothes. They hadn't been wearing that much to begin with, so the results were interesting. Duke Cyron sent Castle Ranit's servants among his guests with pitchers of cooled wine and beer, but took nothing himself. As far as Blade could tell, the old man was hardly even sweating.

Blade didn't hear any more side bets now. Everybody was either out of money or becoming cautious. "Come on, Cheeky," Blade muttered under his breath. "You've put on a good show. Now don't ham it up!" He suspected the advice would do no good even if it somehow reached Cheeky. If any living creature was ever a born show-off, it was Cheeky.

The sun rose higher, sweat flowed faster, and the plume on Duke Padro's hat began to droop. So did Posass's feathers. Cheeky's feathers, on the other hand, were hardly long enough to droop, and Blade wondered if his shorter feathers weren't giving him the unexpected advantage of keeping cooler and more comfortable. He'd have to ask after the fight, if there *was* an "after the fight."

Blade was just about ready to call for some beer, when Cheeky stopped running. He caught everyone by surprise, including his opponent. A wild roar of excitement went up all around the field as his dagger flashed in the sun. Posass of Gualdar jumped back, but not far enough or fast enough. His feathers were limp and dark with sweat. Cheeky really had worn him down! His dagger raked across Posass's belly, blood oozed, and the roar from the crowd swelled. Posass struck back, but Cheeky drew his attention with a punch at his face, and the dagger thrust went wide.

The return stroke did not. It came up under Posass's ribs and into his vitals so fast that even Blade barely saw it. But everyone heard the champion of Gualdar let out a wild death scream, spraying blood all over his opponent, then topple over in his last wild thrashings. His agony soon came to an end. Cheeky pulled out his dagger, wiped it off on the body's feathers, then stepped back and began fastidiously trying to clean the blood off himself.

Blade wouldn't have believed that the crowd could make more noise than before, but it did. If a battery of artillery had gone into action in the field, it would have been lost in the din. Blade saw a hard-faced Duke Padro stepping forward to pick up the body of his champion. He was clearly determined to preserve his dignity at least, now that he'd lost everything else.

Slowly the roar died down. Cheeky ran back to Blade and jumped up on his shoulder, squeaking excitedly. Blade imagined a mental picture of Cheeky living the rest of his life in luxury and hoped the Feathered One heard it. Duke Padro knelt and carefully wrapped the body of his dead champion in a silk cloth.

He was just handing the body to his Master of the Feathers, when Duke Garon of Ney strode forward. Ignoring his ally, he stamped up to Blade. The Englishman quickly looked to right and left, to make sure his Guardsmen were there and alert. Garon's eyes had a malign look to them. He resisted the temptation to draw his sword. Let the enemy make the first move.

"That fight wasn't lordly," said Garon, in a voice that sounded like a blacksmith's file putting an edge on a sword. "Your Feathered One was drugged."

Cheeky *yipped* angrily. He might not understand the words, but he seemed to understand that he was being insulted. Blade scratched his back to calm him, without taking his attention off the angry Duke. "I should like to know where you heard that," he said politely. "Someone has been spreading tales."

"Tales!" Duke Garon spat in the dust at Blade's feet. Out of the corner of his eye Blade saw Alsin about to signal the Guardsmen forward. He caught the Marshal's attention and shook his head sharply. Using the Guards would mean a general riot and much unnecessary bloodshed.

"Yes, tales," said Blade. "And whoever spread them is as much your enemy as he is mine."

"You—!" Garon gobbled like a turkey, unable to get out words for a moment. "You're calling me a liar, aren't you?" he said finally.

Taking up this challenge would mean giving Garon his choice of weapons, but Blade couldn't see that there would ever be a better chance to push him into a duel. "Yes," he shouted, raising his voice so that as many people as possible could hear. "Duke Garon says the champion of Nainan was drugged. I say he lies!"

"And I say that you, Blade of Nainan, have spoken words against the honor of a Lord." Garon started to take off a glove before he realized he wasn't wearing any, fumbled for something to throw at Blade's feet, and finally wound up spitting again.

This finally broke Duke Cyron's calm. He stared at the Englishman as if he'd grown a second head. Blade was glad Miera was nowhere around. This unexpected duel was news he'd rather break to her himself.

Then the crowd was raucous again, some people cheering, some jeering, some just shouting for the sake of making a noise. The Lords of the Crimson River loved a good fight above anything else, and now they were going to get two of the best for the price of one visit to Castle Ranit!

Eventually the shouts died enough for Duke Cyron to make himself heard. "Duke Padro!" he shouted. "Since there is a dispute over the lawfulness of Nainan's victory today, I will ask no payment on the Duke's wager until the duel of Duke Garon of Ney and Lord Blade of Nainan is fought. Do you consent?"

Padro's voice was steady. "Yes, I do."

"Well and good. I also ask that any others who have won today not ask for their gold until the Fathers have given their judgment in this duel. To do otherwise would be setting our own judgment ahead of theirs, an unlordly thing."

There were murmurs of agreement all around Blade, although some sounded a trifle reluctant. The reluctant ones had probably hoped to make their fortunes by collecting on those twelve-to-one bets!

Blade also noted that the Duke's regard for the Fathers didn't extend to the point of promising not to collect his winnings if Blade lost. Duke Cyron was not a man to carry either piety or confidence in his Captain's fighting ability too far.

Chapter 15

The duel would take place in two days. The delay gave Duke Cyron time to bring in all his fighting Lords from outlying parts of Nainan. It did not allow any of his guests to call up their own reinforcements.

It also gave Blade enough time to make certain arrangements with Chenosh and the blacksmith who'd pointed his sword. He discussed those arrangements with no one else, not even Duke Cyron. Instead he played the part of a man who'd talked himself into a duel he might well lose, but which he must fight because it was his lordly duty to do so.

The worst part of the next two days was keeping up that pose before Miera. He would have given a lot to be able to tell her, and knew that she would hold her tongue. But he also knew that she was no actress, and couldn't possibly keep up the necessary pose under dozens of pairs of sharp eyes. So he kept his mouth shut and endured her tears, her anger, and her back turned to him in the bed at night. By the customs of the Crimson River he was entitled to beat her black and blue for this disobedience. He only hoped his not doing this wouldn't cause too much comment.

He wasn't as forebearing with Miera's grandfather. The Duke cornered him one evening after dinner, wished him luck, praised his courage, and added, "I hadn't expected such a good chance against Duke Garon this soon. Since we have it, you must not throw it away. I tell you plainly,

104

it is more important that Duke Garon of Ney die than that you live."

Blade had expected this. After all, he was *still* an outlander, still as much pawn or tool as ally. Also, he agreed with Cyron. Duke Garon had thrust himself into a completely unnecessary fight at the worst possible time for him. He ought to pay the price of being so quick-tempered. Blade thought of the saying, "Never give a sucker an even break." However, he wasn't going to give the Duke the satisfaction of agreeing. Instead he fixed the old man with a cold stare. "Is that so? I am sure Miera would be interested to hear it."

Then he turned away, leaving the Duke as close to gaping helplessly as he could be. Cyron loved his granddaughter and even valued her goodwill as much as any Lord on the Crimson River could value the goodwill of a woman. Reminding him that Blade could ruin his reputation with Miera could do no harm.

The duel would take place at dawn, to spare the horses from doing hard work in the heat of a summer day. The early hour didn't reduce the crowd. When Blade led his charger out onto the field, there were already more people around it than he'd seen at the monkey duel. Many more of them were Lords or Helpers wearing Duke Cyron's colors. The old Duke was too honorable and too wise to be plotting against his guests. He was also determined to make sure all the fighting today would take place on the dueling field.

Chenosh was doing Helper's work for Blade, with Lord Gennar assisting in any job which needed two good hands. Lord Gennar wasn't in on the secret of Blade's plans for the duel, but felt he owed him this honor, and Blade trusted him to keep quiet if he guessed anything.

Blade waited until Duke Garon rode Kanglo out to his end of the field, then pulled his helmet on. Gennar tightened the thongs which held it to his shoulders, then helped him mount. Chenosh stepped forward to hand him his lance, the first of three to be broken "in honorable coursing upon horseback." If the duel wasn't decided by one of the three lance breakings, the jousters would fight for half an hour on horseback with sword or mace and shield. If there was still no decision, they would dismount and continue the fight until one fighter yielded or was disabled. Blade had no intention of letting things go on that long.

Trumpet calls, drum rolls, and cheers all rose as Blade rode out onto the field with his lance held high. The pennant Miera had embroidered for him fluttered just below the gleaming steel tip. He was glad she was watching him take it into battle for the first time. Unfortunately she'd come out to watch more from fear of scandal if she didn't appear than out of respect for him. Perhaps by the end of the day she'd be in a more forgiving mood.

Then Blade put everything out of his mind except the stocky little man on the huge chestnut horse a hundred yards away.

Silence fell, to be broken by the three trumpet blasts signaling, "Get ready." Blade lowered his lance into striking position, thrust his feet deeper into the stirrups, and gripped the horse more tightly with his knees.

Two trumpet blasts—the "Get set" call. Kanglo whinnied as his rider's excitement reached him, and the horse pawed up clods of earth.

Then a single long trumpet blast—"Go!"—and Blade crouched low behind his shield as he spurred his own horse forward.

Before they'd gone ten feet Blade's world magically shrank. The crowd was gone, its cheers no louder than the distant whine of a mosquito. Sun and sky overhead were gone, and so was the earth underfoot. There was nothing left except the horse under him, its animal sweat strong in his nostrils, and the fast-growing shape of Duke Garon and Kanglo. He breathed something as close to a prayer as he ever did, then the two jousters met.

Somewhat to his own surprise, his lance actually struck the Duke's shield. It was a glancing blow, which gouged the shield's leather covering and sent his lance darting off at such an angle Blade barely held on to it. Duke Garon's lance struck square, and Blade's shield was split halfway through and slammed back against his chest. Only his mail coat and arming doublet underneath saved him from cracked ribs. Only his firm seat on his horse kept him from being flung backward out of his saddle. His horse was thrown back on its haunches, while Kanglo shot past, hardly missing a step.

Blade rode down the field to Duke Garon's end before turning back for a new lance and shield. Everyone there was cheering the Duke's victory in the first coursing and jeering the poor showing of the outland Lord. Blade saw Duke Padro standing in the crowd surrounded by his guards. For a moment their eyes met. Then Blade turned his quivering horse and urged it gently back down the field.

The second coursing went almost the same way as the first. Blade's lance struck closer to the center of Duke Garon's shield and broke. The Duke struck even harder than the first time, and for an ugly moment Blade thought he was going to lose his seat. He kept it only through his abnormally good sense of balance. The cheers and jeers from Garon's side were even louder, and Blade thought he heard a few rude remarks about "outland Lords who think they can fight mounted'" from his own side.

He rode back to his own end and dismounted, while Chenosh let the horse drink and Gennar handed him the third lance. Blade ran his eyes quickly up and down the twelve-foot shaft, saw everything was as it should be, and mounted again.

The loudest roar of all went up from Duke Garon's people as the jousters rode out for the third coursing. Their Duke had taken the first two. This time he'd not only take the coursing but put an end to that upstart Blade of Nainan!

Blade grinned and spurred his horse forward. This time he only got it up to a trot. He wasn't going to have much room for error even at a trot. At a gallop he'd have none at all.

Kanglo and his rider grew steadily larger. Blade's eyes fed their images to his brain, and he calculated the shrinking distances with the precision of a computer. The two riders were forty feet apart when he leaned far over to one side. To everyone who saw, it looked as if he was losing his balance or even that his saddle was slipping. Garon had the chivalry not to strike at a temporarily helpless opponent.

He raised his lance and swept past. The moment his opponent was clear, Blade flung himself out of the saddle, as though he was fainting or the saddle girths were broken.

The moment he was clear of the horse he let go of his lance. It would take all his skill and reflexes to fall safely in his heavy armor. If he had to keep one arm busy with the lance, he'd probably break something at a time when even a sprain could be fatal.

The lance flew into the air like a rocket as Blade fell. The noise from Duke Garon's cheering section was deafening. It didn't fade even when a thousand pairs of watching eyes saw Blade roll clear of his horse's hooves, then bounce to his feet. As the Duke reined Kanglo to a stop and turned him, Blade covered the forty feet to the fallen lance and snatched it up. He quickly ran his hands down the shaft. It was ready.

"Lord Blade," the Duke shouted. "Do you yield?" Blade raised the lance high in both hands, then shook his head. "Very well," said the Duke. He raised his voice. "Lord Blade refuses to yield, though he is unseated. I claim my right under the laws of the duel."

That right was to ride Blade down where he stood.

Blade's taunting reply was lost in the roar of the crowd, with the Duke's people cheering again and the men of Nainan shouting in rage and horror. Garon backed Kanglo away to give him more room to gain speed. Blade moved his hands up and down the lance into carefully marked positions, then put it over his knee. With a sudden twisting of arm and shoulder muscles, he snapped the weapon where the blacksmith had sawed the shaft partly through, tossed away the butt end of the lance, and raised the rest. It was now the exact length and balance for a throwing spear.

If Duke Garon ever realized this, no one else ever knew. He was probably too excited at seeing an easy victory over the man who'd insulted him waiting for him almost at the end of his lance. If so, this excitement was the last feeling he experienced in his life.

The Duke lowered his lance and dug in his spurs. Kanglo surged forward. Blade's arm rose, the spear point gleaming in the sun. Then he threw. Duke Garon hadn't bothered to lower his head behind his shield. That would look like cowardice, against an opponent who couldn't strike back effectively.

The improvised spear took him squarely in the mouth.

Instead of the roar Blade expected, there was an awful silence as Kanglo charged past, his rider dead in the saddle. The force of the blow drove the bloody point out through the back of Duke Garon's skull. He swayed but didn't tumble to the ground until Kanglo sensed something was wrong and suddenly reared. Then his rider fell with a thud, Kanglo squealed like a mad thing and bolted, and the silence of the crowd broke. Surprise, joy, anger were all in the cries. Blade thought he heard the sound of weapons clashing as well, and hoped that Duke Cyron's Guardsmen had the situation in hand. He bent to pick up the butt end of the lance, then started walking toward his horse.

By the time he was mounted again, Duke Garon's Helpers had removed the corpse and led Kanglo off the field. Chenosh and Gennar ran out to meet the champion. Both of them were grinning so broadly that they couldn't talk at first, but the crowd was still making so much noise Blade wouldn't have heard a word anyway. At last the noise died down to where he could bend down and speak to Chenosh. "I thought I heard some fighting, just after Garon went down. What happened?"

Gennar answered. "Duke Raskod's women seemed to be favoring you. Some of them cheered when Garon fell. Raskod was so angry that he stabbed one. She fell, and another woman came to stand over her. Raskod ordered this woman taken away and turned over to his guards, then drove the rest of the women into their tent." Gennar shook his head. "The women should have known their place, but nonetheless Raskod's anger was unlordly."

"Yes," said Chenosh. He was nodding, but Blade thought he looked oddly satisfied. Before he could reply, he saw Miera burst out of the crowd and sprint across the field at a thoroughly unladylike pace. She was holding her skirts up and displaying a scandalous amount of leg. Obviously she didn't care and Alsin was too busy elsewhere.

Miera ran up to her husband's horse, but the crowd was bellowing again, so that he practically had to read her lips

109

to understand that she was apologizing for doubting him. After a minute he bent down, scooped her up, and plopped her into the saddle in front of him. She was showing even more leg than before as they rode back to where Duke Cyron was waiting for them.

By nightfall, Duke Cyron had settled one way or another with all three of his guests.

Duke Raskod and his household were on their way home, by Cyron's orders and with fifty armed and mounted Lords escorting them. Neither Cyron nor his Lords cared much about the women who'd been killed (the one turned over to the guards had also been killed). But they did care about getting a Duke who could lose his temper in such an unlordly way out of Nainan as fast as possible.

The men of the late Duke Garon were also on their way out of Nainan, as fast as they could go without leaving their leader's body behind. It was no secret that they were in a hurry to return home to their share of the spoils in the civil war which now loomed on the horizon as Garon's four sons fought over his Duchy.

Duke Padro of Gualdar stayed behind at Castle Ranit. In return for being forgiven all but a token payment on his wager, he swore allegiance to Duke Cyron and his heirs in all matters of peace and war for the space of five years. He swore this oath by the Fathers and by everything else any Lord or priest in the castle could remember being used to swear on. Bound by so many strong oaths, he could now betray Cyron only at the price of being outlawed and having his Duchy confiscated.

"He may even be sincere," said Chenosh to Blade after the oath taking. They were sitting in the older man's chamber, along with Alsin and Miera. Blade hadn't witnessed the oath taking, being busy patrolling the castle grounds with a force of mounted Guardsmen and dismounted Helpers. "Certainly he was greatly relieved not to lose his Duchy. It will be months before he recovers his wits enough to think of plots. By then we may have our work done."

Blade frowned. "We only have one of the four Duchies we needed on our side."

Alsin snorted. "Now that Duke Garon is dead, Ney is as good as in our hands. The only question is not whether we can take it, but how much of it will be left when we do. Garon's sons will be four scorpions, stinging each other and everyone within reach."

Chenosh nodded. "And as for Duke Raskod—he may find enemies where he does not expect them. I have done my best to see that he will, by paying a little visit to his harem." He stood up, dropped into a stooping posture, and said, imitating Blade's voice, "Lord Chenosh, may I offer you—oh, sorry."

Blade stared, then laughed. The merchant on the road *had* been Chenosh, wearing makeup and a false mustache, and somehow he had persuaded Raskod's women to go against their Lord. "So you can disguise other things besides Feathered Ones, Chenosh?"

"Yes, although I never had to masquerade for such high stakes before. Still, I don't think any of Raskod's women recognized me."

Alsin frowned. "Are you sure? Begging your pardon, but your hand—"

"Come, come, Alsin. Most of the things I did with the women did not need two hands."

Miera giggled and Alsin looked scandalized. "Chenosh, guard your tongue. Your sister is present, and it is unfit—"

"Oh, go tie yourself into a knot, Alsin. My sister is a married woman. She should know what we are talking about. Or do you mean to suggest Blade is so lacking in manhood that he has not taught her?"

At this point Miera started laughing so hard she finally had to stuff her hair into her mouth and bury her face against her husband's back to stop herself. Alsin turned away, and Blade could have sworn the Marshal was blushing.

Chenosh sat down on the bed, poured himself more wine, and continued quietly. "The women who died today were not the first to suffer at Raskod's hands in that way, but they may well be the last. I have given their comrades some weapons, to pay the blood debt when they think the time is ripe." Then Chenosh explained what the Lords of Nainan were going to have to do.

Chapter 16

In Duke Raskod's castle, Issos, the woman called herself Sarylla. When she'd been a free blacksmith's daughter she'd used another name. No one else alive knew it, and she herself forgot it for months at a time. Tonight it was very much in her mind. After tonight she would be free—with either the freedom of a living woman escaped from slavery, or the freedom of a dead woman escaped from everything in the world.

She and the other women of Raskod's harem had just returned to Issos after their sojourn in Nainan, and they were now going to do something about their plight. For too long, the Duke and his Lords had abused them, but the brutal killing of two of their number in Nainan had been the last straw. Now, with the weapons they had been given by the mysterious stranger in Nainan—not to mention the other "thing" he had given them, which made them feel like real women again—they were prepared to get control of the castle and put an end to their slavery once and for all.

Before they left Nainan, they had worked out a plan with the stranger. Sarylla and the other women would take over the gate tower that controlled the drawbridge, and then they would hang out signal lanterns. A messenger from Nainan would be watching, and he would immediately report back to his Lords, who would then ride into Issos and force Duke Raskod's men to surrender the castle.

Then there was Duke Raskod himself, but Fara, who was at present his favorite bed partner, had come up with a plan to do away with him. She was going to poison him, then take her own life, screaming out at the same time to let the others know the deed was done. Sarylla had tried to protest, but Fara raised her hand to silence her "My life is a small thing to give in exchange for the lives of our women," she said. "It will be done as I have described," and her tone indicated that she would tolerate no argument.

So the two women embraced and wished each other well, then left Nainan with the weapons concealed in their voluminous capes and gowns. Meanwhile the stranger had returned to his own people, to arrange his end of the bargain.

Now Sarylla reached the door at the foot of the spiral stairs inside the gate tower. The guard who should have been standing there was nowhere in sight. She breathed a short sigh of relief and motioned her friend Elcha forward. They stood by the door, almost holding their breath as they listened for the sounds which would tell them they had even less time than before. "If you hear—what we are sure to hear," said Sarylla, "call the others forward at once and bring them up the stairs. I don't care what you've heard or not heard from me. Bring them."

Elcha laid a hand against Sarylla's cheek. She was ten years older than her leader and looked almost old enough to be her mother. She still followed the younger woman because her combination of fiery courage and cool thinking made Sarylla the most worthy of the castle's women to lead—next to the one who would not live through this night, whatever might happen to the rest.

Sarylla slipped the fine-bladed dagger deeper into her red silk trousers and hurried up the stairs. The guard who should have been at the bottom was at the top. He sat on the floor with his back against the wall, his mace across his knees, and a jug of wine ready to hand. He only raised the mace when he saw the woman standing over him.

"Huh. What are you doing here, girl?"

"Well . . . Would you be telling the Duke or the House Mistress if I told you?"

"Maybe, maybe not. Depends on what you pay me." His leer made it obvious what sort of payment he expected. Duke Raskod seldom objected to Lords taking his women, but the hired guards were another matter. They seldom got the taste of a clean, good-looking woman.

"I can pay it if we're quick." Sarylla started unfastening her tunic and tried to get a look into the next room, where the machinery for controlling the drawbridge was stationed. From the shadows, it looked as if there was only one other guard. That would be enough to end her life, but not enough to hold the tower against the other six women. Even if there were the usual four guards in the tower, it would be best to go ahead. The worst death the guards could give them would be better and quicker than the deaths they would face otherwise.

The guard stood up but didn't take off his clothes. He only leaned back against the wall and fumbled with the lacing of his trousers. At the same time his eyes were devouring Sarylla's bare breasts. So he wanted her to suck him, did he? Better and better. She wouldn't have to strip completely, with the trouble that could give her in keeping her steel hidden.

She crawled over to the guard's feet on her hands and knees, a position which she knew made her breasts swing interestingly. Then she half rose and went to work.

Sarylla didn't have the most skilled mouth in Castle Issos, or at least Duke Raskod said so, and she supposed he knew what he was talking about. However, the guard wasn't Duke Raskod, and Sarylla quickly had him groaning with pleasure and thinking of nothing else except her hot lips on his manhood—sucking, licking, dancing up and down his shaft all the way to its root and then back down to the sensitive areas near the head. . . .

Sarylla knew that in another moment he would grip her by the hair while she finished her work. That would destroy her freedom of movement. She slipped her free hand inside the waist of her trousers and came out with the knife. The guard had his eyes closed, so he never saw the steel. He only felt it searing his skin, sliding between his ribs into his heart. Life went out of him in the same moment as he reached his climax. Blood and other fluids mingled in the pool spreading around him on the floor.

Sarylla leaped up as he crumpled, spat furiously to get his taste out of her mouth, then leaped through the door

114

into the main room. The guard there was just rising to his feet with a suspicious look on his face. She snatched the oil lamp off the table and threw it in his face. He leaped back, but found his way barred by the winch handle. Before he could draw his sword Sarylla was on him, stabbing at throat, chest, groin, thigh, and everywhere else she could reach. She was that most terrifying kind of opponent, one who doesn't care if she dies as long as she can kill. The guard was too overwhelmed to strike back until he had lost so much blood that he lacked the necessary strength for this task.

Sarylla left him dying on the floor, ran back to the head of the stairs, and shouted down. A shout from Elcha below answered her, then more shouts from the other women.

As if to echo the shouts came a woman's scream of mortal agony. A terrible silence followed, lasting just long enough to let the women at the foot of the stairs hurry through the door, close and bar it, then scurry up the stairs. Suddenly shouts and running feet began to fill the castle as Duke Raskod's Lords realized what was afoot.

Quickly the women went into the room and pushed all the furniture in it down the stairs to make a pile against the bottom door. The guards' bodies were stripped of their weapons and clothing and sent after the furniture. Then they closed, locked, and barred the upper door and slumped to the floor. They were breathing heavily and sweating partly with the effort, partly with stark fear at their own boldness.

Sarylla was the first to rally. She forced herself to stand up, take a few deep breaths, and look out the window. Nothing was happening in the village at the foot of the hill—not yet. The news of Duke Raskod's death would be all over the castle by now, but someone would surely have sense to keep it inside the gates for now. However, the watching eyes in the village would be enough, once they hung out the signal lanterns. . . .

"The lanterns!" Sarylla screamed. If they weren't ready to hand . . .

Elcha laughed and pulled two of the horn-and-brass battle lanterns out from under her cloak. "I had them with me all along," she said.

115

"I'm sorry." Sarylla pushed sweat-dampéned black hair out of her eyes. "I suppose my thoughts were elsewhere."

That provoked a laugh which raised everyone's spirits. It didn't take long to get out the third lantern, light all of them, and lower them out the window on lengths of rope. With the signal lighted, the women were now free to explore their improvised refuge. Some were frightened to discover there was only a day's supply of water in the tower. "If the Nainans don't come soon, we'll die of thirst," one wailed.

Elcha flayed the weaklings with her tongue. "Even dying of thirst is a better death than Fara's," she snapped. "If you're afraid of that, you can always jump."

"And if you don't shut up I'll *throw* you out the window," Sarylla added. She said this as much to beat down her own fears as to impress the other women. Every time there was a silence, she found herself listening for more screams—the death screams of anyone who came in the path of Raskod's men. Then she bit her lip. She'd be no sort of an example to the others if she didn't get a better grip on herself. She peered out the window, to see if the lanterns were burning steadily, then turned back to the others.

"Let's get a file and start sharpening all the weapons," she said. She bent over to pick up the mace and only then realized she was still naked to the waist. And her tunic was now on the other side of a locked door.

Oh, well. If the Nainans come in time, I'll be glad to greet them stark naked. If they don't, I'll be too dead to worry about clothing.

A good many eyes were watching the castle from the village. All saw the three lanterns hung out of the gate tower and wondered what they meant. Only one pair of eyes belonged to someone who knew.

That man waited just long enough to count the lanterns twice. Then he mounted and rode for the border of the Duchy as if monsters were snapping at his horse's heels. His horse was a good one, but it was lathered, staggering, and more dead than alive by the time he crossed into

116

Nainan. A few miles farther on, it finally collapsed and died, but by then he was within sight of one of the frontier castles. By noon his message was on its way to Marshal Lord Alsin, and Captain of the Guardsmen Lord Blade was waiting with three hundred mounted Lords in the forest south of the castle.

By nightfall, the three hundred Lords had crossed into the Duchy of Issos and were riding hard for Duke Raskod's castle.

It took Nainan's Lords two days to reach Castle Issos. By then they knew that the message had told the truth. Duke Raskod was dead. The poison he'd sucked off Fara's nipples had done its work. In every village and from every castle they passed, they heard this. They also found so much confusion that nobody could have opposed their march even if he'd wanted to. In fact, most villagers and some Lords openly welcomed the riders of Nainan and the end of Duke Raskod's harsh and pleasure-loving rule. Blade noticed that this kind of welcome seemed to increase in strength the closer they got to the castle.

"The castles and villages close to Raskod's seat were the ones who had to give up their pretty girls for his pleasure," said Alsin as they rode down the last valley before the castle. "He was only able to keep them at all inhabited these last few years by killing anyone who tried to flee. Even Lords sometimes suffered."

Now that Duke Raskod's hand was lifted, the villagers were proving the truth of Alsin's statement by fleeing in swarms. The riders of Nainan covered the last few miles to the castle over roads choked with refugees, carrying babies and valuables and driving livestock before them. All of them seemed to have only one thought—to get out of reach of Raskod's Lords before they started seeking a ghastly vengeance for their Duke's murder. Blade listened to some of the refugees' talk as he rode past. None of them seemed aware that they themselves could make the slightest difference to what happened now.

No two Lords in Nainan's army agreed on what they expected to find at Castle Issos. Personally, Blade expected to find the heads of the women of Raskod's harem on pikes outside the closed gates, with a defiant garrison inside ready to fight to the last man.

They found the gates closed, all right, but they also found the women snugly in possession of the gate tower, able to lower the drawbridge any time they wanted. Under a flag of truce, Blade and Lord Gennar rode to within shouting distance of the gate tower. A lovely young dark-haired woman leaned out the topmost window, bare to the waist.

"Well done!" Blade shouted. "How are you?"

"We're safe for the moment," she said in a cracked, rasping voice. "But for the love of the Fathers, get us some water!"

Blade sent Lord Gennar back to order up pack horses carrying water bags. From the castle walls one of Raskod's men shouted, "You aren't going to help those bitches!" and emphasized his opinion by throwing a spear. It narrowly missed Blade.

He leaned out of his saddle, pulled the spear free of the ground, then shook it at the castle walls. "The next thing any of you throws, the ladies are going to lower the draw-bridge. We'll come in, and we'll come with swords in our hands." Blade wasn't sure if he had the right to make that threat, but he didn't care. The women had shown a cold-blooded courage he greatly admired, and they weren't going to die now that safety was so close if he could do anything about it.

Raskod's men seemed to believe the threat. The men on the walls watched in silence as the women hauled the water bags up to the window. Blade and Gennar were about to ride away when they saw Chenosh riding toward them, escorted by half a dozen Lords. One of them carried a hunting crossbow. Just beyond a spear throw from the wall, the archer dismounted, cocked the bow, put a bolt in it, and shot the bolt over the walls. Chenosh rode up to Blade and explained.

"That's our terms. If they surrender by dawn tomorrow, Duke Raskod's healthy son will inherit the Duchy. He and his Lords must swear the same oaths as Duke Padro, but that's all. If they don't yield, the women will lower the drawbridge and we'll storm the castle. The Duchy of Issos will become part of Nainan."

Blade laughed. "I just threatened them with about the same thing if they didn't let me get water to the women." They turned their horses and rode side by side away from the castle. Blade couldn't help looking back once or twice at the massive walls and the frowning keep. Getting inside the walls would be only half the victory. He hoped that in saying he would storm the castle, Marshal Alsin hadn't made a threat he couldn't hope to carry out.

The men of Nainan spent an uneasy night. Most of them didn't even bother taking off their armor, and no one slept without a weapon close to hand. They ate well, off the sheep and pigs that had strayed from the fleeing villagers, and the smell of roasting meat and the sizzle of dripping fat filled the camp.

First light brought no word from the castle, but it did bring two unexpected sets of reinforcements. One included thirty Lords of Nainan, led by Lord Ebass, the man whom Blade had fought just after his arrival in this Dimension. Still apologetic for having mistaken Blade for an enemy, Lord Ebass was escorting Miera and Cheeky. Alsin didn't dare abuse Miera in Blade's presence, but he did start to question Ebass rather sharply.

Miera stopped him from doing even that. "Ebass knows he owes my husband a service," she said coolly. "I told him that he could pay his debt by gathering some Lords and bringing me and Cheeky here. His honor demanded that he do as I asked, so do not find fault with him."

Lord Ebass had been a man of few words even before his fight with the Faissan Lord had disfigured his face. Now he seemed to be a man of no words at all. He merely nodded and gave a grunt, which might well have been the word "Yes."

The other reinforcements were even less welcome, although not even Alsin dared to say a word out loud against them. They were fifty mounted Lords from the elite companions of Duke Pirod of Skandra, the best fighting leader among the Dukes of the Crimson River. "We have heard of the work of Duke Cyron against his enemies in recent

119

days," said their leader. "Our Duke sent us to see that work with our own eyes."

That was all he would say, and although Duke Pirod was supposed to be Cyron's ally, these uninvited observers made the Lords of Nainan uneasy. There were too many of Nainan's secrets they might learn too soon, but there was also nothing at all to be done about it. Revealing secrets would be bad, but breaking the alliance with Duke Pirod would be far worse.

Whatever Duke Pirod's men hoped to do, the first thing they actually did was to force the surrender of Duke Raskod's castle. Seeing two Dukes now in the field against them, even the most determined and loyal Lords of Issos realized that victory was no longer possible. Defeat might come slowly if they held out, but it still would come, and afterward they could expect no mercy. Also, Duke Raskod's healthy son, with a handful of chosen Lords, had sneaked from the castle and fled the Duchy, just after his father had been murdered. So a white flag rose on the keep, and minutes later the ladies in the gate tower let the drawbridge rumble down. All around Nainan's camp the trumpets sounded "Mount."

As Blade was preparing to lead his Guardsmen into the castle, Miera and Lord Ebass rode up. Lord Ebass was as tongue-tied as ever, but the embarrassment on his face told Blade what Miera must have asked of him.

Why not? thought Blade. *There is no law or custom against it, that I've heard of. Just the bloody Crimson River notion that women should stay home!*

So Lord Ebass fell in with the Guardsmen, and the trumpets sounded again. With Cheeky on his shoulder and his lady beside him, Blade rode over the drawbridge and into Castle Issos.

Chapter 17

The flight of Duke Raskod's son left everything in confusion at Castle Issos. After hearing of this, Duke Cyron appointed Chenosh his viceroy for the Duchy of Issos. Chenosh would live in the castle, with a force of two hundred armed Lords under Blade's command. He would have no power of "high justice"—life and death—but he could judge all other cases brought before the ducal court.

Everybody knew but nobody said this wasn't just an effort to get government in Issos working again. It was also a test for Lord Chenosh, to see how fit he was to rule.

Chenosh had only a few days to play ruler before his grandfather arrived to plan the rest of the war. All he could do in that time was put Castle Issos into some sort of order. He buried the dead, dismissed untrustworthy servants and those who'd been cruel to the harem women, laid in supplies of food and wine, and counted Raskod's treasure. He left much of the work to Blade, who left a good deal of it to Miera. She'd helped run Castle Ranit since she was fourteen, and had a keen eye for a falsified account or a dishonest servant.

Lord Gennar was also a great help to Blade, and so was Sarylla, the woman who'd spoken to him from the gate tower. Gennar and Sarylla spent so much time in each other's company that Blade couldn't help joking with the Lord about it. Gennar replied earnestly, "I want to understand this woman. She must have a rare soul, almost lordly, to have done what she did. Yet a woman with a true Lord's soul would have died before entering Duke Raskod's house at all. I do not understand her, but I want to."

Blade managed not to smile again. More simply, Gennar was young, unmarried, and lusty. Sarylla was beautiful and available. Blade suspected that she would have been quite happy to crawl into his bed if he hadn't brought Miera with him. Since he wasn't available, she would try to insure her position by sleeping with his second in command.

Blade wished them well. He hoped Gennar would learn something more about women from Sarylla. Certainly he and the other Crimson River Lords needed the knowledge!

The day Duke Cyron reached Castle Issos, it looked as if he'd brought half the Duchy of Nainan with him. The rest of the Guardsmen were with him, several hundred other Lords, as many Helpers, all the unlordly except for the men and boys needed to keep up a war camp, and several dozen Feathered Ones. No women, though. When Cyron took the field himself, he turned a cold eye on camp followers. As he told Blade:

"The fewer comforts my Lords can bring with them, the harder they'll fight to get back to what they've had to leave behind."

Other men weren't as realistic. Duke Padro of Gualdar came with Cyron, bringing a hundred fighting Lords and his usual tentful of perfumed fops. He was a subdued and sober young Duke in spite of this, seldom speaking, and looking as if he wasn't sleeping well. Escaping from total ruin through the mercy of his enemies had taken something out of the man, or perhaps put something into him which hadn't been there before.

There were also a hundred more Lords from Duke Pirod of Skandra and a hundred and fifty from Cyron's other ally, Duke Ormess of Hauga. The Lords of Hauga came with a lengthy pack train of wine and women, along with their good horses and sharp swords. They spoke quite plainly about why they'd come. "Duke Ormess knows he has to aid Cyron in the fight against his enemies. Otherwise Cyron will be able to say, 'What did you do for me, that you deserve a share in what I have won?'"

The plots and intrigues were going to get thicker and deadlier as Duke Cyron approached final victory. Just as obviously, matters would be even worse if Nainan's three victories had taken months instead of weeks. The Lords of the Crimson River would never know how much they owed to an "outland" Lord, a Duke's one-handed grandson, a proud Feathered One, and seven gallant concubines.

The allies would be marching against Duke Klaman of Faissa with the strongest army seen along the Crimson River in generations. They would have more than a thousand Lords and an equal number of Helpers, counting only the fighting men. Duke Klaman would be lucky to put seven hundred fighters into the field. In a pitched battle, the allies would have no trouble.

Things would be different if they had to lay siege to Castle Muras, Duke Klaman's seat. It was the strongest fortress along the Crimson River, almost impossible to take by storm. It would also be hard to lay siege to it. By now Duke Klaman must know what was going to happen to him. He'd be laying in enough supplies to hold Castle Muras until either winter, or possibly the army of one of the Kingdoms, came to his rescue.

"Is there a quick way to victory?" was the question on everyone's lips when Cyron's council of war met in the great hall of Castle Issos. Blade had no chance to speak for quite a while. Cyron first took the advice of Padro of Gualdar and the chief Lords sent by other Dukes. Then he took the advice of his own Captains, in order of their length of service to him. He was a long time getting around to Richard Blade, who sat through all the nonsense as patiently as he could.

When his turn came, Blade had to start off by asking a question. "What are the buildings like in Castle Muras? What are they made of?"

The best answers came from Lord Ebass, who'd visited Muras several times, and from Chenosh, who'd read everything written on the subject and committed most of it to memory. It sounded to Blade as if the buildings of Castle Muras were very much like those of the other castles he'd seen along the Crimson River.

"That means they'll burn easily," he said. "If they burn, all the supplies and most of the shelter for Klaman's fighting men will go up with them. With no shelter and short rations, how long will the garrison be willing to hold out?"

Everyone seemed to agree that the garrison would yield quickly. That was the answer Blade expected. The Lords of the Crimson River were used to fighting cheap wars, with small stakes. They wouldn't manage very well if suddenly, with no warning, someone raised the stakes by burning their roofs over their heads.

It was Marshal Alsin who asked the next question. "How are you going to set the buildings of Castle Muras on fire?"

"We shoot flaming arrows over the walls," replied Blade simply.

There was a collective gasp, and everyone stared at Blade as if he'd just said something obscene. Then there was an uproar like a barnyard full of animals running wild. Blade mentally kicked himself. He'd overlooked the taboo on using archery against men of lordly rank. He hadn't actually forgotten it, he'd just assumed that no one would think that the use of flaming arrows against buildings would break the taboo. Apparently he'd overestimated the intelligence of the other Lords.

After the council recovered from the shock, they did Blade the courtesy of explaining in detail why his proposal could not be accepted. Again it was Alsin who spoke, with the others all nodding as if he was expressing profound wisdom instead of probable doom for Duke Cyron's cause. "Close to the wall, the archers would be within spear-casting distance. They would die before the fires were well started. If they stand back where they will be safe, they cannot aim well. They might hit a Lord by chance. Then the Fathers and the other Lords would turn against us and all our hopes."

Blade gritted his teeth. He was tempted to ask if Alsin preferred losing the war in an honorable, lordly way, to winning in a new way. He fought the temptation, because he already knew the answer. It would be "Yes," and if someone as comparatively sensible as Alsin would say that, there was no hope of getting a different answer from anyone else!

Once again, Chenosh came to Blade's rescue, although this time he needed a little help. "Your Grace," he said, looking at Duke Padro. "I have heard tales that there are some powerful crossbows in your castle. They shoot far-

124

ther, straighter, harder than any other bows in the lands of the Crimson River. Are they still fit for use?"

Duke Padro's mouth opened like a dying fish, and for a moment he seemed uncertain whether to answer or not. Then slowly he nodded. "Yes. In my father's youth, we had a plague of wild boars. He had two dozen big crossbows made, to kill a boar at four hundred paces. They proved their worth."

"And you still have them?" Chenosh prodded.

Padro hesitated again, but not so long this time. "Yes. If you think they could be used . . ." He didn't know what to say next, or if the other Lords would even approve what he'd said so far.

Blade took up the fight. "I think Duke Padro's bows will do the work," he said. "If they shoot four hundred paces, the archers can stand out of spear range from the walls and still hit anything in the castle. Also, they will be shooting straight. If we choose good archers and bid them aim true, no Lord will be hurt. Not unless he tries to pluck a bolt out of the air, at least!" That got an encouraging laugh.

"What do you say, my Lords?" Blade now asked. "It is the law, not to deliberately shoot an arrow at a Lord or near him. But does the law say we must also protect our enemies from their own stupidity, as if they were little children too young to be let outdoors without a nurse?"

"It has never said that, in all the years *I* have been obeying it," said Cyron.

"That is my thought, too," said Alsin, and Duke Padro nodded. With these three supporting Blade's interpretation of the law, no one else seemed ready to argue. The discussion quickly turned to the best way of carrying out the new plan for burning Duke Klaman out of his castle.

That still took hours, because every Lord wanted it on record that he'd made *some* suggestion. Few seemed to care whether the suggestions made any sense or not. Blade began to feel that staff conferences were the same in every Dimension—a golden opportunity for long-winded drones and a complete waste of time for everyone else.

The council of war finally ended when both Duke Cyron's temper and the beer in the cellar of Castle Issos ran out. Fortunately they'd made most of the necessary decisions by then, and agreed to turn the rest over to Alsin and the Captain of Duke Pirod's elite companions.

Blade controlled a sigh of relief as he left the hall, then controlled a groan as Lord Chenosh scurried toward him. The boy was assigned to ride with the baggage trains and serve with the archers. There was no way he couldn't be resenting it, and no way Duke Cyron, Alsin, and Blade were going to change their minds.

Blade still managed to listen to Chenosh patiently for about five minutes, as the young man complained that he would be so far in the rear he wouldn't get to see any action. Then Blade broke in sharply, "All of what you say is true only for a pitched battle in the open field. If that happens, you will indeed be somewhere else.

"But if we strike fast enough, we will be under the walls of Castle Muras before they even know we are coming. Then the archers will be doing the real work. Attacks from the castle will come straight at them. If you stay with the archers, you'll see enough fighting to keep any man from questioning your courage." *And much more than your grandfather will like,* was Blade's unspoken conclusion.

"You are sure of this?" said Chenosh. For a moment he seemed no more than an uncertain boy, as nervous about his honor as the most thick-skulled Lord.

"I have seen it happen in several sieges on my travels," said Blade. "I cannot promise more than that."

"Thank you, Lord Blade," said Chenosh with a sigh. "At least I can trust you never to tell me more than you know to be the truth. I wish I could be sure of that from anyone else." He walked away slowly, his shoulders sagging.

Blade went back to his room muttering to himself. By the standards of the Duchies, Chenosh and Miera were both adults, but that didn't mean they'd learned more than a fraction of what they needed to know. They were still absurdly young for the responsibilities they already had to bear, never mind what might be thrust on them soon!

Blade was glad to find that Lord Gennar and Lord Ebass wanted a drinking companion. In his present mood, almost any excuse to get drunk would do, even if there were nothing left in the castle but sour wine!

126

Chapter 18

Once you gave Marshal Alsin orders, he would work all day and half the night to carry them out. He might have doubts about new methods of warfare. He might raise ridiculous objections about minor points of law. He might be fussy about honor. But he understood the importance of speed in warfare, and Blade knew that could make up for a lot of other vices.

It also helped that the first attack against Duke Klaman and Castle Muras would be made by an entirely mounted force. Alsin wouldn't try a regular siege unless the fire arrows failed. So he wasn't going to take wagonloads of food, beer, tents, and spare weapons for the first attack. The stewards at the various castles of the alliance would be collecting all these supplies, of course, just in case they were needed. But the first attack on Duke Klaman would lay in the hands of a thousand picked riders, riding fast and striking like a summer thunderstorm.

"We can be even more sure of surprise if we go through the hills to the north," said Duke Padro one evening over the wine. "I have men among my guards who were—well, let's be honest. They were outlaws in those hills. They know the trails and paths."

Blade considered the idea. He trusted Duke Padro now. The young Duke was so eager to get back some of the reputation he'd lost over the monkey duel that he and his courtiers were working like galley slaves. "I like the idea," he said finally. "Alsin, what about you?"

The Marshal frowned. "We can certainly go places with

horses we could never go with wagons. But will this take longer? To keep surprise, we'll have to hurry."

According to Padro, there were several trails in the hills. They chose one which would take only two days longer than the most direct route to Castle Muras. It would bring them out of the hills onto the banks of the Crimson River only a few miles north of the Castle.

It took Nainan's attacking force five days to reach the northern borders of the Duchy of Faissa, and two more days after that to reach the Crimson River itself. This was the first time Blade actually saw it, after months of living in the lands named after it. He was surprised to discover that the name was no exaggeration. The river really was a deep crimson. He asked where the color came from.

As usual, Chenosh gave the best and most complete answer. "In some places the color comes from the sand of the bottom. The sand is crimson, and the color flows out like dye from a pot. In other places, the color seems to be in the water itself. A scholar who wrote on plants two centuries ago said that it came from tiny plants living in the water."

Probably a form of fresh-water plankton, taking its coloring from the mineral salts washing out of the sand in the bottom of the river. Blade wished he had the equipment to analyze the mineral salts, but realized that he'd have no time even with the equipment. They were less than a day's brisk riding north of Duke Klaman's castle. They had to push on now or lose all chance of surprise.

Toward mid-morning they came to the Narrows of Glin, a place where the hills came down almost to the river bank. There was only room enough for two horses to pass abreast. A handful of men could hold it against an army, even without bows. Alsin sent Blade forward with Gennar, Ebass, and two hundred Lords, to scout the countryside beyond the narrows. Such a force could snap up any small enemy patrols and warn of the approach of any larger force. Meanwhile the rest of the army could water their horses, oil their weapons, then come through the narrows ready to move straight on the castle.

There were places in the narrows where men of Blade's vanguard had to dismount and lead their horses. Nevertheless, the whole two hundred Lords got through and were

128

riding south before noon. As they spread out again, Lord Gennar moved his horse in close to Blade's. He seemed uneasy, and Blade thought he knew why.

"How was Sarylla when you left?"

Gennar started so violently he nearly fell off his horse, then frowned. "I have to keep telling myself that you do *not* read men's thoughts," he said finally. "Otherwise . . . Sarylla was well. And I am glad of that. More glad than I ought to be. I am a Lord, and I cannot properly care so much about Sarylla."

"Why not?" said Blade. He suspected that Gennar was in love with Sarylla and needed help to stop feeling guilty about it, help that Blade could give. Whatever Gennar and Sarylla did after that was their own business.

"Why not!" exclaimed Gennar. "She is not of lordly birth. Her father was a blacksmith. She herself has lived— as she has lived—rather than die. So I am not even as sure as I once was that she has a lordly soul in her woman's body. Yet—I wish her well, I wish more of her company. Her company pleases me. . . ."

Blade held in his laughter, but Gennar's situation was not at all amusing to the Lord himself. So Blade said quietly, "Are you so sure that Sarylla's choosing life in Raskod's household rather than death at once proves she does not have a Lord's soul? Remember, in the end she chose to risk that life to destroy her enemies and aid her friends. How can you be sure she did not plan this from the first? It takes a Lord's strength and courage to live a shameful life so that you can take a better vengeance in the end."

Gennar frowned. "I never thought of that. Could it be so?"

"We see it that way in my homeland. There are many tales of warriors who played the coward until their enemies were no longer on guard, then struck." Blade hoped he would not have to make up more than a few of the "many tales." He didn't think he would. Gennar was willing to believe the best of Sarylla, as long as a Lord he respected told him it was all right to do so. In spite of his years and proven courage in battle, in some ways Gennar was hardly more than a boy.

Blade was halfway through his storytelling when he

heard a trumpet sounding. He looked up to see two of the scouts riding back at a gallop. One was bleeding and both horses were lathered. The wounded man galloped up and gasped out his report.

"Duke Klaman's men. They're out on the riverbank, coming north fast. All of them. All!"

"There can't be *all*—" began Gennar.

The scout snarled. "I know what I saw, and what killed two of us. Five hundred at least. If Klaman has any more I've never heard of them."

At this point Blade held up a hand for silence. In the silence they all heard it—the drumming of hundreds of horses advancing fast across hard ground. Gennar sighed. "Forgive me, Lord—"

"Never mind that," said Blade. "Gennar, take your wing and ride back to the narrows. Send a few trusted men through to warn our people, and hold the narrows to the death with the rest."

"But—"

"Don't worry, you'll see your share of fighting sooner or later. Ebass and I will take the rest of our men and hold that hill we passed a mile back. The Faissans will be tempted to attack us there, but we can hold for a few hours at least. When Alsin comes up we can catch their Lords in the open field and break Klaman at one blow!"

As long as Blade's plan would still lead to a classic pitched battle on horseback, Gennar was happy to go along with it. He was smiling wickedly as he rode off, bawling orders to his eighty-odd Lords. As they started to pull out of line and follow him, Blade looked south. He could already see the dust rising from Duke Klaman's advancing riders.

"Center, left wings!" he shouted. "Follow me! Every four men count off one as a horse holder. Everyone with an ax, have it ready for cutting trees. Don't worry, they'll be cutting flesh and bone before the day is over!"

Like Lord Gennar, most of the men Blade was keeping with him didn't quite understand what he was planning. Like Gennar, they did know it would lead to a good fight. For the moment that was more than enough for any true-blooded Lord of the Crimson River.

An hour later Blade was bruised, horribly thirsty, and dripping with his own sweat and other men's blood. He also began to think he'd been too optimistic about how long his men could hold out.

The scout certainly hadn't exaggerated the number of the Faissans. Whoever was commanding them had more than six hundred fighters with him. Fortunately Blade and his men reached their chosen hill with a few minutes to spare for building a breastwork of logs and boulders. Dug in there on the hill, they gave Duke Klaman's Marshal a problem he couldn't solve quickly.

Or maybe the enemy leader knew the solution but didn't have enough control over his men to apply it. Certainly he was no Marshal Alsin. The only men under his command who were acting together were the horse holders along the riverbank. Most of these were Helpers, and even some of them kept drifting up to join the battle. Blade saw horses breaking away simply for lack of men to hold them.

Otherwise no more than thirty or forty men seemed able to act together. Certainly no more than that attacked at any one time. Blade's men could easily beat off such attacks. They drove back six before they lost count. In the process they killed or wounded more than their own number of enemies.

It couldn't go on like this, of course. Ten of Blade's men were dead and a third of the rest wounded, although some of the wounded were still fighting. The enemy could go on attacking up the hill until Blade's men were too exhausted to lift their weapons, then slaughter them where they stood. Blade decided that before he'd let that happen, he'd lead the survivors in a charge downhill at the enemy's horses. If he could stampede them, Nainan would win today even if he and all his men died. On foot, Duke Klaman's Lords could never escape Alsin, and the war . . .

Drums signaled another attack. Blade saw that someone among the enemy was finally using his head. About forty Lords were coming uphill together, holding their lances out in front of them like pikes. They might find it hard to get over the breastwork. Blade's men would find it even harder to fight them without leaving the breastwork's protection. Right now Blade would have given his left arm for fifty archers and a chance to turn them loose on the attacking Lords!

He shouted the appropriate orders, although he was beginning to become hoarse. Guardsmen who still had their throwing spears came forward, and also every man with an ax who could be spared from some other part of the line. Blade himself sheathed his sword and picked up an ax he'd taken from one of his victims. It was too light for penetrating armor, but it would chop through lance shafts and maybe break arms very nicely.

The improvised phalanx of Lords came tramping up toward the breastwork. They were chanting a battle song as they came. All around them their comrades stopped their own work, then joined in the song. It seemed to give the attacking Lords new strength. They came up the last few yards of the hill to the breastwork as if they were going to break through or die in the attempt. Blade spat out a mouthful of saliva black with dust and crouched behind his shield. These men might be his last sight on earth, if this was earth. . . .

Suddenly the screaming of scores of horses drowned out the battle song. The attacking Lords stopped as suddenly as if they'd stepped into tar. Blade saw one of his men heave a spear at the enemy and shouted "Hold!" He stood up, ignoring the enemy only a few yards away, and looked downhill.

The enemy's horse lines were churning and boiling like a pot of untended soup. Horses were bolting in all directions, with Helpers frantically running after them or even more frantically jumping out of their way. Dust rose, and mixed with it was a growing amount of greasy black smoke. Blade thought the smoke looked like it came from the fire arrows prepared for use against Castle Muras, but that was . . .

"Look!" Lord Ebass gripped Blade's arm and pointed. Blade didn't quite hear the word, but he understood the iron grip and the pointing hand in the blood-caked mail glove. Out in the middle of the Crimson River, men seemed to be standing on the water. It was too far to make out their colors, but Blade recognized their motions. They were cocking, loading, and shooting crossbows.

A dozen trails of smoke arched across the river, landing among the enemy horses. This time some of the bolts struck living flesh, and screams of pain joined the screams of fear. Blade saw one horse run wildly uphill with its man on fire. It charged into the middle of twenty Lords, scattering them, then lashed out with teeth and hooves in blind agony. The horse killed three men before someone crushed its skull with a mace.

More smoke trails, more screams, more running horses and men, and then a banner rose among the men out in the river. The sun off the water half-dazzled Blade, but he recognized the banner. It was Duke Padro's, and a moment later the banner of Nainan rose beside it.

Of course. A sandbar out in the middle of the river, just below the surface. Chenosh and Padro got out there somehow with the archers. Now they're shooting up Duke Klaman's horses!

There was still no sign of Alsin and the main body, but the attacking Lords were beginning to look nervously behind them. Losing their horses would be an expensive disgrace, even if nothing else happened to make it a disaster.

Blade decided it was time to see about guaranteeing the disaster. Time to mount his men again and lead them out. On horseback Blade and his fighters could easily get between the dismounted enemy and their home castle, pick them off a few at a time, keep them in the field until Alsin came up. . . .

The enemy was off-balance. In war that was always the best time to give him a good hard shove, so that he fell all the way over. Blade started giving orders.

Ebass wanted to lead the attack, and Blade would have let him do so if he'd been able to speak more clearly. Instead he gave Ebass command of the men assigned to open the breastwork and hold it on foot as the mounted men rode out. They went to work, as the Lords of Faissa began in ones and twos and then in dozens to hurry downhill, hoping to catch their horses before it was too late. As he mounted, Blade saw some of them shaking their fists at him. He thumbed his nose back, then waved to his trumpeter.

The harsh brass voice called out "Charge!" Blade dug in his spurs and set his horse at the gap in the breastwork. Ebass waved as Blade shot past and plunged down the hill, with a hundred mounted Lords on his heels.

Chapter 19

It was exciting to gallop down the hill, but Blade started to rein in his horse before he'd gone far. The slope was steep, the ground was rocky, and Duke Klaman's Lords were running about like cockroaches. Some of them were still full of fight as well. Blade saw one stand holding his lance out in front of him until a Nainan rider impaled his horse on it. The horse and both men went down and none of them got up again.

On the level ground riderless Faissan horses were added to the running men. Blade got his horse down from a canter to a trot. He guided it past the bodies of horses struck down by crossbow bolts and Helpers trampled by maddened horses. Flies were already gathering on some of the corpses, but the crossbowmen out on the river were still shooting furiously. Blade raised his pennant and waved it, but with the sun in their eyes no one out there saw it. The stream of bolts continued.

Blade's horse was a steady, intelligent beast. While its rider was trying to signal to his allies, it went on picking its way cautiously through the confusion. By the time Blade gave up trying to signal, he and his mount were both well south of the battlefield. For a minute or two he was embarrassingly alone, a possible victim for any Faissan Lords who noticed him. Then his men started to come up, and he no longer felt as if he were stark naked in Piccadilly Circus.

Blade found himself at the head of more than eighty men. Last among them was Lord Ebass, and Blade was glad to see him. He'd let Ebass take the rear guard because he was the best man for the job. He was also the man Blade would have hated most to lose. Ebass saluted, fell in beside him, and together they led their men off toward Castle Muras.

As they moved out, Blade noticed some of the Faissan Lords had caught their horses and were moving toward the river. It was time for Chenosh and Padro to stop shooting and fall back to the far side of the river or the even greater safety of Alsin's main body. They'd done everything necessary. Blade doubted that Klaman's Marshal would even be able to get his men to the narrows, let alone defeat Gennar before Alsin came up. Duke Klaman's field army would not see another sunset. The only question left was how long it would take to finish off the Duke entirely. The answer to that now lay mostly in the hands of Blade and his eighty riders.

Blade led his riders south until they rounded a bend in the Crimson River which hid them from the battlefield. On the way they saw several small bands of horsemen, who refused to come anywhere near them. They also saw a number of peasant farms lying abandoned. When Lords fought along the Crimson River, the only safety for other men lay in getting as far away as possible.

Once around the bend, Blade reined in and summoned his men to rally around him. "We're going south to Castle Muras," he said. "We'll get between Klaman's Lords to the north and the castle, then keep them from getting home until Alsin comes and breaks them. If we all stay together, we'll be stronger than anyone we'll be meeting the rest of the day."

"What if Klaman's Marshal does bring his people off the field before Alsin comes?" said one skeptic. "Or what if they send out the rest of the Lords in the castle?"

"If Klaman's Marshal retreats, so do we," said Blade flatly.

135

"There's no honor—" began someone.

"There's no honor in getting killed fighting a useless battle against odds!" Blade snapped. "Better to wait a few hours and fight for victory beside Alsin. Or does anyone doubt he'll come?" He glowered at the Lords around him. None would meet his eye after that question. Thank goodness for Alsin's reputation!

"And they will not send out the Lords of the castle," said Ebass. "They do not have enough. If they do, it will be a mistake. We will show them that." This was the longest speech Blade had heard from Ebass since his face wound, and most of the words were badly distorted. Everyone seemed to understand him, though. Perhaps the berserk gleam in his eye helped.

"Are there any more doubters?" said Blade into the silence. The silence continued. "Let's be on our way, then."

Blade's eighty moved south at a walk, to spare their horses. Even the most eager Lord understood the need for that. They might be thrusting themselves into the lion's jaws, and a man's chance of even dying with honor could depend on keeping a sound horse under him.

They rode so close to the river that Blade's mount sometimes splashed through shallow puddles. Out on the river small boats scurried frantically out of spear-throwing distance and fear-stricken men jumped overboard from rafts or logs. On land they passed more villages, bare of life except for an occasional stray dog or chicken.

A mile on they came to a family trying to drive its pigs onto an improvised raft. The pigs scattered with frantic squeals, and most of the family did the same. A small boy couldn't run fast enough to keep up, and after a look back, his mother turned to stay with him. She knelt with her son in her arms as Blade rode up, her eyes closed and her mouth twisted in prayers or perhaps curses. Blade fumbled in the purse on his belt and pulled out a handful of silver coins.

"Look, woman!" he said softly. "For your pigs." He had to call three times, and when the woman did open her eyes and look up, he thought for a moment she was going to faint. Then she grabbed the coins as if her life depended on them. Blade rode on, the expression on his face discouraging questions. He hoped the coins would be enough for her pigs. The gift wasn't enough to silence the rage inside him, at the way things worked in this Dimension—or rather, didn't work for anyone except the Lords and their chosen friends. When he looked back a few minutes later, the woman was back on her knees, but this time she was counting the coins over and over again.

The eighty rode on, through a land so lifeless that the silence and stillness were eerie. Blade found himself looking back over his shoulder again. All he saw were his own riders on their sweating horses and the distant cloud of dust from the battle by the river. Then they came around another bend and were in sight of Castle Muras.

Duke Klaman's seat was the strongest fortress in the Crimson River lands. It stood on level ground, close to the river which filled its moat and let the Duke bring in supplies by boat. Other than the moat it relied entirely on its massive walls for protection. Some years ago, Duke Klaman's father tore down part of his keep, used the loose stones to strengthen the walls, and turned what was left into a pleasure palace.

From those walls and the palace roof floated a number of brightly colored banners. From a mile away, Blade couldn't tell if one was Duke Klaman's. He could definitely make out something much more important.

The drawbridge was down.

In fact, not only was it down but the gate was open. As Blade watched, he saw three ox-carts rumble out of the shadowed gateway, across the bridge, and onto the road along the moat. It looked like "business as usual" at Castle Muras, with no one suspecting what was going on barely five miles away.

The last stronghold of Duke Cyron's enemies lay open to Blade and his eighty mounted Lords.

He quickly gathered his men around him. Speaking softly, fighting the absurd notion that the enemy might overhear him from the distant walls, he gave new orders. They would form two lines, then advance at a steady trot, as if they were Duke Klaman's men with every right to be riding up to his castle. They would hold back to a trot until

137

they were challenged, then take the drawbridge at a gallop.

Once inside they would start by setting fire to everything which would burn. That should destroy the supplies and make it impossible for the castle to stand a long siege. After that, it would be a simple matter of "kill or be killed."

"I will praise every brave deed. I see," Blade concluded. "But I am going to be busy enough myself. So do not worry about whether I see you. Only remember that you will be able to tell your grandchildren that you were with Lord Blade and Lord Ebass, the day they took Castle Muras!"

He'd struck the right note, so much so that he had to stop the men from cheering him. Then they formed the two lines and were off again. Blade found himself thinking more kindly of the Lords of the Crimson River. For all their faults, they would follow a leader they trusted into hell and out the other side. Right now that particular virtue outweighed a lot of their faults!

Three-quarters of a mile. Half a mile. A quarter of a mile. Blade began to measure the distance to the castle gate in yards. Three hundred yards, two hundred—if there was much archery in these lands, they would now have been within bowshot. For once the laws against using archery against Lords would work in Blade's favor. The men on the walls wouldn't dare shoot at riders who were certainly Lords, whatever else they might be.

A hundred and fifty yards, and a trumpet call came from the wall. Blade's trumpeter replied. The riders closed another fifty yards in silence. Then a human voice took over.

"Who goes there?"

"Lord (mumble) of (mumble)," replied Blade. "Bringing a hundred men to Duke Klaman's service for the war against Nainan." Those words took him across another ten yards.

"Who?"

Blade repeated the garbled identification, and added, "Has Duke Klaman marched yet?" That was good for fifteen yards.

"Yes," the man on the wall shouted. "They rode north

this morning, to catch Nainan's men coming through the narrows. . . ." The voice trailed off into silence. Blade took a deep breath and grinned at Ebass. Ebass returned the grin as well as his scars would let him. Then . . .

"Nainans!" screamed the man on the wall. "To arms, to arms, to guard!"

The scream was as good as a trumpet call for Blade's men. Some of them were off the mark so fast they'd got ahead of their leader before he could even dig in his own spurs. Then his trumpeter sounded and the whole band plunged forward toward the castle gate.

Blade and Ebass wanted to be the first riders in through the gate. It was not only their duty as the leaders; it would also give them more control over the battle inside the castle. But it was a vain hope. Everyone was racing toward the drawbridge as if his fortune depended on being the first inside. Blade stopped trying to take the lead and started trying to keep the frenzied riders from crashing into each other. Then he had to stop that, too, and concentrate on keeping his own legs from being smashed by other horses cannoning into his.

The drawbridge was starting to rise as the first riders charged onto it. Under their weight it slammed back down, chains, snapping and lashing about like giant whips. Someone inside the castle tried to lower the portcullis, the iron grille just inside the great iron-bound wooden gates. It came down halfway, then impaled a Nainan rider and his horse and stuck. The opening was too low to let a mounted man pass through, but more than a dozen riders already passed beyond it.

Blade reined in desperately, trying to avoid smashing into the portcullis at a gallop. He had almost succeeded when his horse lost its footing on the dung-slick stones of the gateway. The animal crashed down and Blade fell clear, feeling as if all his bones had been jarred loose. He couldn't get up in time to save his horse from a castle defender who ran forward and crushed its skull with an ax, but when at last he did get up, he drew his sword and beheaded the man before he could escape. Then he threw his shield in front of him and joined the men who'd made it through the portcullis. The defenders couldn't have dropped and died much faster if they'd been machine-gunned.

There was a battle fury in Blade and all his Lords, and this was not the day for ordinary men to stand against them and hope to live.

When the fight around the portcullis was over, Blade was able to look back toward the drawbridge and the open ground beyond it. Most of the riders were luckier than he'd been. They'd not only reined in but kept their seats. Now they were leaping to the ground, drawing their weapons, and hurrying forward to join their leader. Horses were wandering free, and a few were swimming in the moat, but all the men were coming on, fit and ready.

As Ebass joined Blade inside the gateway, war cries echoed around the courtyard. Then a mass of men appeared, armed but mostly unarmored, launching a hastily improvised counterattack in the hope of staving off disaster. Blade and Ebass joined six Nainans backed against the portcullis and got ready to hold on to the death when suddenly, screams and the clash of steel sounded from directly overhead. A moment later three bodies came hurtling down, castle defenders with their throats cut. The portcullis itself let out a terrible squeal and groan, then began to rise.

"We've got the gateway," roared Blade, so loudly that men standing next to him flinched. "Come on, and we'll have the castle!" He whirled his sword around his head in a gesture of pure bravado, then charged forward into the ranks of the enemy.

Blade wasn't sure if he gave any orders after he came to sword strokes with the castle's defenders. Certainly his men did everything he would have ordered them to do, whether or not he ever said a word. So he was free to hack his way through steel and flesh, until the cover was stripped from his shield, the edge was gone from his sword, and he was red from head to foot with other men's blood.

Ebass fought beside him most of the way, his twisted mouth open to let out the sort of battle cries heard in nightmares. Ebass seemed determined to kill ten of Duke Klaman's men for every tooth he'd lost in his battle with the Faissan Lord. If he didn't succeed, it was only because after a while none of the castle's defenders would stand against him.

From the gateway Blade and Ebass fought their way to the door of the palace, while the men behind them scattered in all directions to kill and burn. By the time the two warriors were fighting five Lords at the palace door, smoke was pouring out of the kitchen hut, the stables, and one of the storehouses.

Normally, five men should have been able to hold a flight of stairs against two, but this wasn't a normal fight. Blade and Ebass killed three opponents in as many minutes and drove a fourth over the side of the stairs. He broke a leg in the fall and was stabbed where he lay. Then the men inside the hall opened the door to let in the last defender. Ebass threw a spear, catching the man in the throat. He fell, blocking the closing of the door. Blade dashed forward, picked up the fallen man's ax, and used it to kill two men trying to drag the body clear. Three more ax blows on the door and it was sagging on its hinges. It would stand against dogs and thieves, but not against fully armed Lords with the strength of madmen.

Blade and Ebass charged through the door, running so fast that one defender died simply by falling down and being trampled underfoot. Then they had a clear view to the end of the hall. A lean, gray-haired man in silvered armor was sitting on a chair of carved stone with polished brass fittings.

"Duke Klaman," said Ebass, and got ready to charge. Blade held him back with his shield, raised the ax, and started swinging it around his head. As Duke Klaman started to rise, Blade threw the ax. It flew the fifty feet separating the two men, struck the Duke in the chest, and tore through his mail as if it were cardboard. He dropped back into his chair of state and died sitting there, blood forming on his lips.

"They will call you Duke-Slayer," said Ebass, looking from the man to his victim.

Blade shrugged. The battle rage was beginning to pass off. He was aware of new bruises and freshly pulled muscles, the smell of blood and smoke, and all the things which still had to be done to consummate the victory. His men were inside a castle still held by three or four times their number. Blade pulled his ax free of Duke Klaman's chest, dropped a scrap of cloth over the dead face, and led Ebass out of the hall to rejoin the battle.

There wasn't much battle left to rejoin. The hurricane-swift eruption of Blade's men into the castle inaugurated the collapse of the defender's morale, the defeat of the counterattack continued it, and the word of Duke Klaman's death finished the work.

So the castle was well in hand, and all the defenders safely locked away, even before the first reinforcements rode up just before sunset. Fifty mounted Lords, in battered armor and on lathered horses, brought word that nearly all of Duke Klaman's field army was either dead, captured, or fleeing for their lives. Blade sent a man on a fresh horse from the castle's stables back to Alsin to take word of the Duke's death. Then he put the new arrivals on guard duty, so that his own riders could finally get off their feet and put down their weapons. Few of them were unwounded, and none of them had the strength left to raise a soup spoon, let alone a sword or mace.

Shortly after dark new reinforcements arrived—Duke Padro and Chenosh, with the men who had stood with them in the river and an assortment of companions from Skandra and Lords from both Gualdar and Nainan. Padro put himself and his party under Blade's command, giving him more than two hundred men to hold Castle Muras through the night. Blade would have been content, except for the news Chenosh brought. "King Fedron of the East Kingdom intends to march on the lands of the Crimson River," he said. "The word came just as we were rounding up the last of Klaman's men."

Clearly King Fedron realized that if ever there was a time to attack, that time was now. Even though Cyron of Nainan had won victories over all the hostile Dukes, the lands of the Crimson River were in great disarray, and its Lords could be overwhelmed by the Eastern Kingdom's superior forces.

That was an unpleasant but undeniable possibility. Blade

looked around at the sprawled bodies and charred ruins, and listened to the wailing of women and the screams of the wounded. The fall of Castle Muras wasn't going to end the fighting along the Crimson River after all. There were other and probably bloodier battles to come.

Chapter 20

The news of King Fedron's invasion nearly drove out of Blade's mind another question he'd been asking himself. The man shouting from the walls of Castle Muras had hinted that the Faissans knew the invaders were coming and the route they were using. Was this so? If it was, how did they learn? Blade considered the possibility of spies among Duke Cyron's men. It was an ugly thought.

He had no chance to mention it until breakfast the next morning. All they had was salt beef boiled with something like rotten horseradish, but he was too hungry to care. When his stomach was quiet, he raised the question with Alsin and Chenosh. He was glad Duke Padro had gone to bed, or he couldn't have spoken so freely. Padro could be trusted, but what about all his men?

"None of the four Dukes we fought would have hired spies in Cyron's household beforehand," said Alsin. "Padro and Raskod were too lazy. Garon trusted us, although he did not like us. Duke Klaman trusted no one, but preferred to rely on the strength of his walls and fighting Lords. He would have considered it cowardly to waste money on spies."

Blade hoped Alsin's judgment of their four opponents was correct, but even if it was, that didn't eliminate the danger. "There are Orric's friends, and there may be others

143

who have some grievance against Cyron we can't even guess. Could any of them have given the information to Klaman, just out of hatred of Cyron?"

Alsin and Chenosh seemed ready to fall asleep in their chairs. They'd been driving themselves as hard as Blade, and he hadn't slept for thirty-six hours. "I realize we'll have to ask a few questions around Castle Muras," Blade added gently. "But I think those questions ought to be asked as soon as possible." He poured out some more wine for the other men, but none for himself. If he drank another cup, he too was going to be ready to doze off. "Now, Chenosh, tell me how you and Duke Padro came to our rescue."

Chenosh seemed to wake up at the chance to tell of his day's fighting. "It was really Duke Padro's idea," he began. "As soon as we heard where the Faissan horses were, he came to me. He said he knew of a sandbar in the river within easy bowshot of the horses. With the river this low, the water would be only knee-deep at most. If we crossed the river at the nearest ford, we could move down the far bank. Then it would be an easy swim to the bar."

"How did he know of the bar?" said Alsin.

Chenosh grinned. "He said he'd once had a lover from among the Lords of Klaman's household. They used to meet on the sandbar."

So the archers and a handful of Gualdar's Lords slipped across the river and marched south. Alsin kept a stony-faced silence as Chenosh told of this. Blade knew he must have argued with the young Lord, trying to persuade him against risking his life in such a gamble, but stopped short of provoking a quarrel.

"We came to the place nearest the sandbar. We only had to swim about fifty paces. Most of our men could do that. Those who couldn't, held on to the leather bags of oiled fire wads. They floated well. The archers greased their bows beforehand, and put their bowstrings in their caps."

They'd reached the sandbar without any difficulty, without even being noticed by the Faissans. "All their eyes seemed turned toward you and your men, Blade. So the archers strung their bows, and each took aim at a horse. Padro and I gave strict orders that they should do this.

Archers are unlordly, and some are lawless as well. Then they started shooting, and the rest you saw and heard for yourself."

Blade nodded. "You and Padro saved us, and perhaps the whole battle. Well done, both of you."

"Yes," said Alsin. "But you and Padro defied me. Also, you might have driven the Faissans back into Castle Muras if Blade hadn't seen so quickly what he had to do. You needn't think you're ready for a place in the front of the battle just because of today's work."

Chenosh looked angry. Blade headed him off by asking Alsin for an account of his day's work. The Marshal was as proud of his work as Chenosh was of his, and took much longer to tell about it. Blade was particularly interested to learn that the Feathered Ones were no use in a battle of this size. Only the combat-trained ones had been taken along, and most of these either went mad and attacked their own people or simply ran off and disappeared, when they weren't trampled to death under the horses' hooves. Alsin was annoyed at this but not much surprised—he saw no reason to assume that a battle with more than a thousand Lords in it would be anything like a battle with no more than two hundred. Blade was glad to know Alsin was thinking ahead this way.

By the time Alsin was finished, Blade was barely awake enough to congratulate him. He was never sure quite how he made his way to the bed, where he slept right through the rest of the day.

Alsin immediately began to try to determine how Duke Klaman had learned of the approach of Nainan's army. He questioned scores of men, imprisoned dozens, and even tortured a few. All he could learn was what he and Blade already knew.

"I begin to think that whoever knew the answers has slipped through our fingers," he said after three days. "Perhaps he is dead, or perhaps he has fled beyond our reach."

"Or perhaps he is refusing to answer even in the face of torture, because he knows he'll be rewarded," said Blade grimly.

"Who would reward him?"

"King Fedron," said Blade. "*He* at least must have laid his plans sometime ago. I think those plans included putting spies among the Dukes of the land he hopes to conquer."

Alsin looked uneasy. "Blade, I think you are starting at shadows."

"Do you? Well, you may think that if you wish, but guard your back while you do so. Meanwhile, Duke Cyron will have returned to Nainan by now. I'm going to ride back to Castle Ranit and lay this matter before him. I want to see if *he* says I am starting at shadows."

Cyron didn't think Blade was starting at shadows. He also didn't think there was much to be done about it, even if Blade was right.

"I am not being careless or foolish, either," he added. "So do not say that I am, at least until you have heard me out." Under other circumstances, Blade would have been amused to see the old Duke justifying himself to the "outland" Lord. Obviously Blade was now an ally, even a trusted adviser, and not a pawn.

"We could not hunt down those enemies easily, perhaps not at all. Certainly we could not hunt them down without searching each of the four Duchies we have won to our cause. Such a search would cost time and gold, spread terror, and shed blood. It could make enemies where they did not exist before. In the end, matters might become worse rather than better."

Blade had to admit the wisdom of that argument, but wasn't going to give up. "At least take some care for yourself and Miera. I think you should pull at least part of the army back from Castle Muras to guard Castle Ranit."

"We have enough men here to hold Ranit against any surprise attack," Cyron replied. "If King Fedron sends an army against us, there will be more than enough warning of its coming. Until then, it is better to keep our Lords gathered at Muras, in one place, under one Captain, ready to move as one body."

That also made a certain amount of sense, but not

146

enough for Blade. He still thought Cyron was running foolish risks. He didn't say that, though, for fear that Cyron would think he was asking him to appear cowardly. Then the Duke would turn a completely deaf ear to his arguments on everything, for days or even weeks.

Blade decided instead to try working on Cyron through Miera.

He found her nearly as deaf to what he considered reason as her grandfather. It didn't help matters that she was also pregnant.

"If you did not put the child into me on our wedding night, it could not have been many nights afterward," she said with a giggle. "I do not know if I should hope your loins remain so strong or not. If they do, there will be many fine children to rebuild the House of Nainan. But I should have to bear all of them. I know I should rejoice in the idea like a proper woman, but—"

Blade ran a hand down her bare back and gently patted her buttocks. "You're as proper a woman as any man could wish, and if I asked for more, I'd be a fool." *Why should she look forward to bearing me seven or eight children, then dying in childbirth at the age of thirty?*

"Let us take the children one at a time, as the Fathers send them to us. Let us also finish talking about what I asked you. Will you help your grandfather understand that Castle Ranit is too weakly defended?"

"Too weakly for your peace of mind, perhaps. But if it is strong enough for my grandfather, he will not change his mind. Not even if I asked him, and I will not."

Blade sat up with a jerk. "Why? Miera, this is—"

"It is nothing less than my lordly duty, to avoid seeming weak and fearful. I must do this, or I could be marking our child. Would you have him grow up a coward because I could not sleep without guards outside my door? You do not understand how such things look, through a woman's eyes." She laid her head against his chest so that her silky red hair brushed his stomach.

"No," said Blade with a sigh. "I suppose I do not." *Nor do I understand as much about what it is to be "lordly" as I thought I did.*

Miera moved against him, more insistently. He decided it was time to forget about lurking dangers, at least for tonight.

If Blade couldn't save Cyron and Miera from their own stubbornness, he was determined to save Cheeky. So the Feathered One was perched on the saddle in front of him the next morning as he rode over the drawbridge. Miera waved her scarf to him from the keep window, then he gave his mount its head.

Alsin had set up a system of relay posts running all the way from Castle Ranit to the borders of the Duchy of Faissa. By changing horses at each post, a strong rider could cover what was normally a five-day ride in a single day. Blade compromised, changing horses about halfway. He spent the night at an inn, and reached Castle Muras about mid-afternoon of the next day.

He knew something was wrong almost the moment he rode through the gate. Each man he passed looked intently at him, then quickly looked away, as if afraid Blade would read his face. In the stable it was the same. He also saw a totally exhausted horse with Cyron's brand on it, standing in the stall next to his.

"Would someone please tell me what happened?" he snapped. "Has my face turned purple or something?" He spoke sharply, to drive away the cold doubts clutching at him.

No one answered. Everyone seemed more reluctant than before to meet his eyes. Then he saw a familiar figure silhouetted against the door of the stable. Chenosh stepped forward, and Blade saw that his eyes were red and his face drawn and gray. The doubts were suddenly even more chilling.

"Chenosh, what—?"

"Blade—my grandfather is dead. Murdered. It was yesterday morning, shortly after you left Nainan. A messenger from the castle rode straight through to get here with the news."

"What about Miera?"

"She—she fought the murderer. She—she's hurt, and may not live."

Blade's legs held him up as far as a bench by the door. Then he sat down and swallowed hard. "All right, Chenosh. Tell me."

"It was yesterday morning . . ."

Chapter 21

Miera had come down from the keep, to find her grandfather already at breakfast in his private chamber. He looked her over as she sat down on the far side of the table.

"You are well, Miera?"

"Now don't *you* start fussing over me, Grandfather. I'm going to have quite enough of that from Richard."

"You have told him you are with child?"

"Of course."

"Miera, your tongue—"

She smiled and reached out a hand to him. "Grandfather, forgive me. But I think you must understand that the way I speak to men now is what Richard taught me. I know his way is not the way of the Crimson River, but—"

Cyron threw up his hands. "Now it is my turn to ask you not to fuss. I understand. Very well. Blade's way with women is indeed his own, but I will not say anything against him because of that. A man who fights and leads as he does can be forgiven many faults."

Miera wanted to go around to the other side of the table and kiss her grandfather. But she saw a servant approaching, and decided to wait until he was out of earshot.

The servant was a tall, heavy man, with a bushy head of graying red hair. He announced that six Lords from Gualdar were in the courtyard below but would not intrude on His Grace's meal. Cyron thanked them for the courtesy and promised to receive them in an hour. The servant bent to offer the Duke a raisin-stuffed chicken. Miera thought she saw metal gleaming in the man's hair. Now why should he be wearing a comb like a woman?

Suddenly the man's hands went limp and the chicken on its massive silver platter crashed to the table. Chicken and raisins flew everywhere.

"You clumsy oaf—!" roared Cyron.

"Your Grace, I beg you. Be merciful. I don't know what came over me. . . ." The man clutched frantically at his hair. Suddenly his right hand tightened into a fist, then sprang free of his hair, clutching a long thin dagger. Miera screamed. Her grandfather looked up, just in time to take the dagger in his right eye. She screamed again as he slumped back into his chair, blood running from his nose and mouth. The murderer jerked the dagger free and turned to run.

This made him turn his back on Miera. She hurled herself across the table, her gown snagging on something and ripping to the waist, but she clutched him by the belt. He bellowed and turned, stabbing with the dagger. She felt the steel drive into her back, but it seemed no more than a pinprick. She clutched the belt tighter and started to scream, not in pain but in the hope of drawing the guards.

In this she was successful. But by the time they came, the servant had stabbed her twelve times, then picked up the serving platter and hit her over the head. She was unconscious, and it was not until they'd finished binding the killer that the guards realized she wasn't dead. By that time the "Lords from Gualdar," who'd been planning to cover the assassin's escape, or if necessary finish his work, were riding for their lives. Every Lord in the house who could find a horse leaped into the saddle and chased after them.

"At least the dagger wasn't poisoned," Chenosh concluded dully. "So she may live, if her skull is not broken too badly."

Blade only twisted his fingers together in impotent fury. He wanted to strangle someone with his bare hands, but no one within reach deserved that fate. Even if some-one did, killing wouldn't bring back Duke Cyron or cure Miera.

"Well, Your Grace—" he began, when he could trust himself to speak.

"*Please,* Blade!"

"No, Chenosh. You are now Duke of Nainan. The sooner you accept it and start behaving like a Duke, the sooner your grandfather will be avenged and his work fin-ished."

The youth sighed. "Very well. Then my first order as Duke of Nainan is that you do not call me 'Your Grace.' Now what were you going to say?"

"I was going to ask how many of the assassins do we have for questioning?"

"The killer himself is alive. So is one of the six riders. They caught up with a second, but could not take him alive."

"He was probably the one who knew all the secrets," said Blade sourly. "However, two prisoners are more than I expected. I think you should reward the guards. Soon— while they're still alive to spend the money."

"I will send you back to Castle Ranit yourself, to give them the money and hear what the prisoners say," said Chenosh. *And see Miera.* The thought hung unspoken in the air between them. "I will come—"

"You won't leave this castle without at least a hundred armed Lords around you!" snapped Blade.

Chenosh's face hardened. "My second order to you as Duke of Nainan is not to interrupt me. Let me finish what I have to say. You may find it wiser than you think!"

"I'm sorry, Chenosh." Blade realized just how badly shaken he must be, to have been so rude. Chenosh would need all the help he could get to uphold his authority.

"No harm done this time." Chenosh sighed. "I will re-turn to Castle Ranit as soon as Alsin can spare me enough Lords for an escort. He will command here until I return or send orders."

Blade rose. "I don't know what I might be riding into, at Castle Ranit. So I'll leave Cheeky here, with a message to

151

trust you if I don't come back. If I don't, I think Lord Gennar or Lord Ebass should be given command over the Guardsmen. Both will be obeyed."

"It shall be as you wish, Blade."

"Good." Blade stalked out of the stable. Men cleared a path for him as they saw the look in his eyes and the set of his jaw.

Blade rode back to Castle Ranit as fast as the relays of horses would carry him. He still tried to spare his mounts as much as he could. With war approaching, Nainan and its allies would need every sound horse they had.

He didn't try to spare himself. He ate nothing, drank only water, and said hardly anything to anybody as he pounded down the dusty roads. By the time he reached Castle Ranit, he was a red-eyed, dust-caked figure out of a nightmare.

He found Miera unconscious, lying facedown in the great bed where they'd made love and conceived the child which now might never be born. They'd cut off all her hair to bandage the fractured skull. She looked more like a shrunken doll than the woman Blade had held in his arms no more than two days before.

The doctors assured him of the fact that she was dangerously wounded but that she might survive; certainly they would do everything they could. Blade didn't take much comfort from this. The doctors would try to be optimistic no matter what, and they could hardly promise *not* to do their best. He had nothing to say to them, so he went to look at Duke Cyron's body.

The embalmers were just finishing their work. In the summer heat, embalming was needed to prevent decay even for the few days it would take Chenosh to return for the funeral. With a patch over his ruined eye, Cyron looked as if he'd fallen into a particularly sound sleep after a long day's work. All the servants and even some of the Lords were tiptoeing in and out of the room, and speaking in whispers while they were in it.

Blade spent the rest of the day putting things about the castle in order. The next morning, he awoke to find someone shaking him.

"Lord Blade, Lord Blade!"

"Eh, urmph. What. . . ?" He felt like a bear prematurely wakened from hibernation and only a little more intelligent. Grief, anger, and sheer exhaustion had drained him to the point where he could not spring awake instantly as he usually did.

"Lord Blade! The—the woman Sarylla from Castle Issos. She is here. She says she wants to care for the Lady Miera."

That brought him to full consciousness. "Send her in."

Sarylla must have used the relay stations to get here as fast as she had. She looked as if she'd been dragged by the horses rather than riding them. She didn't want to talk about her journey, saying only that she'd had much valuable help. Blade suspected that she had traded sex for fresh horses, and didn't want to reveal the names of the men. He dismissed the matter from his mind. She had done no harm, and if she could actually help Miera . . .

"I was learning to be an herb woman when my father—was taken away," she said. "After a year in Castle Issos, I became doctor to the women of the household. I treated many stab wounds, and more than a few broken heads, when Duke Raskod or other men grew angry or took pleasure in giving pain. Only two women who were not dead when I came to them died in the five years I did this work. I do not say that I know more than the doctors. I do say that I may know some things that they do not, to help the Lady Miera."

It was grasping at straws, but when there was nothing else to grasp . . . "Go and do your best for her. I will send word to the doctors that they are to treat you as one of their own."

"Thank you, Lord Blade. I hope—I hope I may do work good enough to pay back my debt to you." Now her eyes were on the floor, and Blade could have sworn she was blushing. "How is Lord Gennar?"

"He is well," said Blade. "He should be returning to Castle Ranit with Duke Chenosh in a few days." By the time she turned away, Sarylla was definitely blushing.

* * *

Lord Gennar returned to Castle Ranit with Chenosh four days later. So did Alsin and more than a hundred other Lords. So did Cheeky.

By that time the questioning of the prisoners was finished. For once in his life, Blade was able to sit and watch men being tortured without feeling particularly sorry for them. They'd done something monstrously evil, knowing that it was evil, knowing that it would lead to the deaths of hundreds of innocent people. The only way of saving any of those innocents was to learn everything the guilty ones knew.

By the time Chenosh returned, Blade was able to inform him that at least three of the six mounted "Lords" in the plot were friends of Orric. They'd won over the servant who struck the actual blow by promising to pay his debts to a money lender. The man had been desperate, so afraid he would have to sell his daughters to a brothel to raise the money that he'd been easy game.

The guilty "Lord" died under the torture, and Chenosh had his body thrown to the dogs. The servant was hanged, and after this execution, Chenosh led the way to the Sacred Grove for his grandfather's funeral.

Like Blade's wedding, Duke Cyron's funeral rites were performed as quickly as law, custom, and the dignity of the House of Nainan allowed. The priest threw the torch onto the pyre less than an hour after the body was laid there. As he joined in the Chant for the Dead, Blade again saw the flames light up the metal reflector behind the altar. He'd hoped to return to the Sacred Grove and speak with the priest about that reflector, thinking that perhaps the old man could tell him something about its origins. *Was* it, as he suspected, part of a spaceship which brought the Feathered Ones to this world?

But now that he had returned to the Sacred Grove and the priest was within earshot, asking about the reflector was the furthest thing from Blade's mind. Lord Leighton would doubtless grumble when he heard that Blade put respect to the dead of Dimension X before research for the Project. Let him grumble. Lord Leighton had never fought among a strange people, never risking his life and shedding his blood for them, never loving one of their women and obeying one of their leaders until he felt himself one of them. He could not understand how such things seemed to Blade.

At the council of war after the funeral, Chenosh announced that he would ride to seek aid from King Handryg of the West Kingdom. "The murderers did not name their paymaster, but if it was not Fedron of the East I will be greatly surprised," the young Duke explained. "Handryg has a name for hardness and quick temper, but not for base, vile treachery. Also, we will be helping him to strike at the East Kingdom while it is least expecting it. He may take his payment for the war from the Easterners, rather than from us." He smiled. "I hope I will not sound unlordly if I say that we should not pay more for King Handryg's help than we must."

Some of the Lords did not understand, but no one seemed to be disagreeing out loud. Blade was pleased. If Chenosh had reasoned out this decision on his own, he was taking charge very well. If he'd had advice, it was good advice.

Now it was Alsin's turn. A hundred Lords of Nainan and fifty of Skandra would ride with Chenosh into the West. "We cannot spare more from the battles to come. That will be enough to keep any lesser Lord of the West from treachery against our Duke. As for King Handryg, we can only pray to the Fathers to make both his heart and his steel true."

Blade knew there was a good deal more they could do than pray to the Fathers. He also knew what the council would think of a proposal that had been forming in his own mind: to arm the peasants in the land the same way the Kings armed their peasants. That way the united Duchies of the Crimson River would have a lot more troops of their own. But Blade also knew that if he were to attempt to lead such a peasant army he would spend the war in prison. Better to stay free and do what he could for the villagers quietly, when no Lord was looking over his shoulder.

This didn't keep him from laying some plans now, in the quiet hours of a sleepless night. He rose early, to stand beside Alsin on the roof of the keep and watch Chenosh ride west under the usual cloud of dust. Then he went down to the arsenal and asked the blacksmith who'd made his trick lance for a count of all the spare weapons in the castle which a man on foot could use.

It was a pity he couldn't bring Romiss the Breeder into his plans. The Breeder was probably the best leader among the non-Lords of Nainan and might be willing to tell Blade the secrets of the Feathered Ones, in payment for Blade's trust. But Romiss had also served Orric, the man whose friends murdered Duke Cyron and crippled Miera. Blade wouldn't trust him that far.

Then, of course, there were Blade's own Guardsmen. These men were an impressive fighting force in their own right, even without a peasant army.

As he left the arsenal, he passed a shadowy corner where Lord Gennar and Sarylla stood. Gennar's arm was around her shoulders, and he seemed to be talking earnestly. Blade smiled, for the first time in what seemed like months. If Lord Gennar had so far set aside his rank that he could fall in love with a blacksmith's daughter who had a "lordly soul," he also might see reason—or at least see "lordly souls" in other villagers besides the woman he loved.

Chapter 22

Invaders from the Eastern Kingdom descended into the lands of the Crimson River, wreaking havoc as they pillaged and burned the villages. The war had begun in earnest, and Blade and his men were doing everything in their power to hold the invading force at bay until Chenosh returned with reinforcements from the Kingdom of the West.

Now, however, leading his riders across a little river in the outlying lands of the Duchy of Nainan, he was cautious. The river was swift flowing, and after the rains of the last few days it reached the knees of the horses. With fresh mounts this wouldn't have been a problem, but there wasn't a fresh mount in the whole band.

How long was it since there had been? *Too long,* Blade thought, and shook himself back to alertness. There were bands of King Fedron's Eastern raiders in the area, possibly a danger but also possibly victims. Either way he had to be watchful.

Beyond a fringe of woodland on the far side of the river was a village. The enemy had been there before—*some* enemy. A small village like this was easy prey for one of the invading bands and could just as easily fall to a band of common outlaws, who roamed freely in the lands of the Crimson River now that war had put an end to whatever degree of order the Dukes had maintained. Although the outlaws seldom dared to attack armed Lords, Blade and his men were still on their guard as they rode through the village.

They saw nothing except the usual roofless houses, charred beams, and the wreckage left by hasty flight or looting. They saw no human or animal bodies, but still inferred that the village must have fallen several days ago. The survivors would have long since slipped back, under cover of darkness and carried away their dead comrades for burial, their dead animals for food.

The riders left the village behind, rode around the hill beyond it, and came to a small castle guarding a stone bridge over another river. The bridge was intact; since outlaws and invaders both had to be able to move freely, they seldom destroyed boats or bridges. The castle, though, was another matter. One gate lay flat in the mud, splintered and scarred, the other hung askew from a single twisted hinge, the top of the keep was smoke-blackened, and crows circled around to bodies that dangled over the battlements.

"The Easterners," said Lord Gennar from close behind Blade, who agreed silently. The outlaws never attacked a Lord's castle. Their survival depended on not losing too many men, and above all on not forcing all the Lords of

157

the Crimson River to unite against them. Only King Fedron's men took castles.

Almost any soldier will learn discipline when his life depends on it, and for weeks Blade's Lords had seen men die through lack of it. At this point they could have given lessons to the Grenadier Guards in Home Dimension. Blade fell back to the rear and watched them ride into the castle courtyard two at a time. When he joined them, some were already dismounting and beginning to search the ruined buildings, while others climbed the walls to keep lookout. Having performed this same act twenty times before, the Lords could do it on a black rainy night, and without a single order from Blade or Gennar.

Blade dismounted, and Cheeky jumped from the saddle to the ground. The feather-monkey, too, had his duties: to search the ruins for living Feathered Ones, who might be able to give information about what happened. Cheeky hurried off, *yeep-yeep-yeeping* in an inquiring manner and stopping every few yards to listen for a reply. Blade wondered if he listened with his mind as well as his ears.

Blade stood by his horse in the middle of the courtyard while his men swarmed through the castle, looking for human survivors, bodies in need of burial, weapons, and food—in roughly that order. He doubted that they'd find much of anything in this castle, which looked fairly well picked over already. There wasn't even the telltale stench of long-dead bodies lying unburied in their chambers.

Suddenly Blade became aware that someone was watching him from the gateway. He turned to see a tall, thin man in a ragged farmer's smock, standing in the shadow of the hanging gate. Blade determinedly refused to admit the idea of ghosts. Either the man was there when they came in, or he'd slipped past the lookouts.

"What do you want?"

"Please, Lord Blade—with your permission—you *are* Lord Blade, aren't you?"

"I am," said Blade.

"I am—speaker—for the village—the village between the forest and the river."

"The burned-out one that way?" Blade pointed, and the man nodded. "Now I ask you again—what do you want?

You will have a much better chance of getting it if you ask quickly."

The man gathered his breath and his nerve, and spoke in a rush. "You are Lord Blade, who is giving the steel to those who are not Lords. Forty men of my village are in the hills near you now. We want steel, to use against the men of the East. We know you are the man who can do this for us."

As he started repeating himself, Blade held up a hand for silence. Several Lords were watching them, but none of them was Lord Gennar, the only one Blade would trust to join in these negotiations. Gennar would hold his tongue afterward, even if he did not approve the man's request.

Blade wasn't entirely sure he approved it himself. Until now, "giving the steel to those not Lords" meant turning his back while the peasants made off with spare weapons from looted castles or dead invaders. This villager was asking that his men be *given* weapons, the same way they might be given shoes, bread, or new plows. He was asking that Blade not just overlook the activities of unlordly men ignoring the Lords' laws, but that he actually do something unlordly himself.

If Blade did what the villager was asking, there'd be hell to pay. Most of the Lords were still afraid of lordly weapons in unlordly hands. Most would be ready to turn against Blade were he to help make their fear a reality.

On the other hand, if he refused the villager's request, the word of his refusal would spread, and the villagers who thought of him as a Lord who knew that they were worth more than their own swine or goats would feel betrayed. Twice, villagers' warnings had saved his men from ambushes, and once, a village had given them food, which saved their horses. This kind of help would dry up if he refused.

At least he could play for time. "My men just came to this castle a few moments ago, as I am sure you know," he said. "We do not even know if there is any steel to use left here. If there is not, we cannot help you. Surely you would not ask us to give up our *own* weapons?"

"Oh no, oh no, oh no," the man gabbled. "Nothing like that. Nothing so unlordly. Nothing at all unlordly." Under other circumstances, Blade would have laughed at the idea that it was more unlordly to take a weapon as a gift from a living man than to loot a corpse. However, he'd gotten the message across. Now to find Gennar and ask him to spread the word—if you find weapons, don't mention it. Blade didn't want the villager finding out anything by accident while he and Gennar were making up their minds.

Over the rattle and thump of the searchers of the castle came a high-keening wail. That was Cheeky, signaling that all the Feathered Ones in the castle were dead, and at the same time mourning them. Blade opened his mind to the Feathered One, the first time he'd attempted this in several days, and for a long moment shared in Cheeky's grief. He found it sometimes helped him to help Cheeky through his pain.

He wondered how Miera was. The last word he received was more than a week old when it reached him, and that had been more than a week ago. Sarylla said that the wounds on Miera's back were healing, although she would bear scars. The head wound seemed worse than they'd suspected, however, and she was still unconscious most of the time. They had not told her about the state of things in the Duchies, and would not. Worry for her husband would surely weaken her, and in her condition, that could mean the end.

Blade broke the mental link with Cheeky and turned his mind to conjuring up various unpleasant deaths for King Fedron. He had just reached boiling oil when he heard a shout from the keep.

"Fedron's men! Coming along the river!"

The problem of what to say to the village speaker about giving his people weapons suddenly vanished, and so in fact did the speaker. Blade peered out through the gate but saw nothing. The enemy must still be too far away to be visible from the ground. He scrambled up the nearest stairs and onto the wall, as half-burned planks creaked ominously under his weight.

From the battlements he could see the enemy, some two hundred men with Fedron's and the East Kingdom's banners floating above them. About half were lancers and half mounted infantry with short swords and pikes. The lancers were coming up the hill toward the castle, but the infantry seemed to be milling about at the head of the bridge without dismounting.

He knew that he and his men were in trouble, serious though perhaps not fatal. They were outnumbered two to one and even with the protection of the castle, this inequality might be too much. After all, these invaders had taken the castle once when it was more defensible than it was now. Yet on the other hand, if despite heavy casualties, his forces could repel even one attack, it might be enough. Fedron's bands seldom stayed for a long, costly fight. They were too far from home.

While Blade was counting the enemy, his men were taking their positions for defense. Some held the horses, others climbed onto the walls, still others piled planks, saddles, and charred sacks in the gateway as an improvised barricade. By the time they were finished, the lancers were dismounting by the castle walls, just out of spear range. The mounted infantry was still down by the bridge.

Then a column of horsemen started filing out of the woods on the far side of the river, heading toward the bridge. Blade stared, and once he had convinced himself that he wasn't seeing things, he felt an unpleasant sensation inside. The approaching horsemen wore the colors of the Duchy of Ney, whose Duke Blade had slain with his own hands, in the contest held in Nainan after the fight of the Feathered Ones. So far, the four sons of Duke Garon had not made an appearance in the war, but now apparently they were coming off the sidelines, to join King Fedron in stamping out Nainan's resistance.

It began to look as if the battle was lost before it began. The best Blade and his men could hope to do would be to sell their lives as expensively as possible.

Gennar's voice came from behind Blade. "Shall I have the men start killing the horses?" Horseflesh would feed them during a siege, and dead horses would strengthen the barricade.

Blade shook his head. "Wait a little. With two bands instead of one, it may take them a while to decide what to do. We may not even be attacked today."

This suggestion quickly seemed to have been overly optimistic. The riders of Ney were already halfway up the hill,

161

between the mounted infantry at the bridge and the Lords by the wall. A big man at its head reined in, and the rest followed suit. As the leader started giving orders, Blade recognized him as the late Duke Garon's Marshal. He'd seen the man at the duel, helping to lead his dead master's steed, Kanglo, off the field, and in fact, he was now riding Kanglo himself. The gnawing sensation inside Blade grew stronger.

Then, as fast as the horses could move, the whole scene changed. The Lords of Ney wheeled their mounts around, facing downhill toward the Easterners' infantry. A score of Lords rose in their stirrups and hurled throwing lances. A dozen struck home, and the same number of Easterners toppled off their saddles. Then the Marshal shouted "Charge!" and his men thundered downhill.

What happened at the bottom of the hill was more of a massacre than a battle. The mounted infantrymen who weren't too surprised to fight at all still had no weapons to fight from horseback. In five minutes the only ones who were still alive were those who jumped from their horses and scuttled off into the undergrowth where the Neyans couldn't follow. The Neyans let them go; they had business elsewhere.

Blade's men helped the Neyans with the Eastern Lords. This was a battle, because the invading Lords weren't too surprised to fight and had the weapons to do so. It still wasn't long before those left alive were surrendering. Most of them preferred to surrender to the Neyans. They might have joined in the war for reasons no one could understand, but they didn't have so many deaths or so much destruction to avenge as the men of Nainan.

The fighting was over before Blade could strike a blow. Afterward he rode out, and under the eyes of both sides and all the prisoners, he calmly drew rein beside Ney's Marshal.

"Ah, Lord Blade," said the Marshal. "Unless you have some claim to these prisoners, I would like to keep them for now. They will make good hostages to assure lordly behavior from Fedron's men, should they reach our Duchy."

The man seemed to take it for granted that Blade would consider the question on its merits, as if Ney and Nainan had been allies for months. Well, what better way to start? Where this would end, it was too soon to tell, but certainly two hundred enemies, who'd been free and dangerous only an hour ago, were now dead or prisoners. Blade didn't believe in looking a gift horse in the mouth, and this was nearly a stableful of them.

"I'd hoped we could take a few prisoners of our own," he said. "King Fedron holds some of our Lords, and I'd like hostages, too. I don't suppose he has any Lords from Ney?"

"Not yet," said the Marshal. Those two words said a good deal. "Come to my camp tonight, and we'll speak more of it."

"Very well." In an effort to get some control over the situation, Blade said, "I suggest you make your camp at the foot of the hill. We'll stay in the castle, and share any food we have to spare." He fixed the Marshal with a sharp look. "I think our men should stay apart, at least for tonight."

"Of course," said the Marshal, as calmly as if they'd just been discussing the weather.

Normally, Blade would have put on his best clothes and weapons and ridden down to the Neyan camp with some kind of ceremony. Unfortunately, weeks of campaigning had left him with no "bests." He walked down the hill, wearing the clothes with the fewest holes and the sword with the fewest nicks on its edges. He wanted to have Cheeky riding on his shoulder, but when the time came to go, the feather-monkey was nowhere to be found. With Blade walked six Lords, all armed to the teeth and carrying several hundred pounds of horsemeat.

The Neyan Marshal met them at the edge of the camp. He sent the meat carriers off to the cook tent and led Blade toward his own quarters. As he opened the front flap of his tent, a high-pitched *yeeeep* from two Feathered Ones sounded from the darkness inside. The Marshal raised his lantern, and the pale yellow light revealed the interior of the tent.

The two Feathered Ones stood on his pallet, the larger one crouched over the back of the smaller. Both of their tails stood straight out, and both of their feather crests stood up. Blade sighed. It wasn't the first time he'd seen Feathered Ones having sexual intercourse, and . . .

Then they pulled away from each other, and the larger one *yeeeped* again, indignantly. Blade stared. It was Cheeky! Then the Marshal got a good look at the other, and let out a roar that made the Feathered Ones leap off the pallet and vanish into the darkness. The Marshal looked at the ceiling and said in a carefully neutral voice: "The female—underneath—she was my bonded one— Hoyla."

In the same tone, Blade replied, "The other one was mine—Cheeky."

There was a long silence.

Then the Marshal laughed and reached out to grip Blade's hand. "Allowing for—oh, different ways of expressing it—I want to say the same thing as our Feathered Ones. Ney and Nainan should stand together against the Easterners until the war is won. If there are any differences to be settled after that, we can settle them without giving outlanders—no, hear me out. You *were* an outlander, Blade. You are now blood and bone and earth of the Crimson River, more than those of us who did not see it was our duty to do as you have done."

There was nothing to say to that, so Blade was silent until the Marshal went on. "We can settle our differences afterward. What do you say?"

"Which of Garon's sons do you follow?"

"None," was the surprising answer. "All of them are more interested in winning the Duchy than in being sure there is a Duchy left for them to win. None of them sees clearly that Fedron is a danger to us all. About half of the Lords of Ney have refused to swear an oath to any of the four sons. They are free to take the field under me. I have about half of those, all who had horses and war gear ready to march."

This information kept Blade from having to commit himself to any of Garon's four quarrelsome sons. "I can speak for the men who follow me," he said. "They will fight side by side with yours against the invaders, and as long as necessary. I cannot make promises for Duke Chenosh or Marshal Alsin. If our alliance proves itself in a few more battles, I don't think they'll reject it afterward."

"Good. Then let us seek those battles."

"Wait," said Blade. "Will your Lords trust *me*? Will they fight beside Lords led by the man who killed their Duke?"

"You killed Duke Garon in fair fight, a duel of his own choosing, in no unlordly way, and you showed much courage," said the Marshal solemnly. Less solemnly, he added, "I think none of us doubted Garon would die that way, sooner or later. It was the death he sought, and surely a better death than he would have gotten from King Fedron."

Blade couldn't disagree with that last point.

When he walked uphill later that night, his stomach was heavy from too much undercooked horsemeat and his mouth was sour from too much bad wine. Cheeky rode on his shoulder, half-asleep, smugly content with his night's work, and stinking to high heaven. Blade still felt better than he had since he heard the news of Cyron's death.

Chapter 23

At the same time as Ney's Marshal was approaching Blade, Marshal Alsin was leading out the forces of Nainan, Gualdar, and Skandra a hundred miles away. Between them, Blade and Alsin cleared the Duchies of King Fedron's bands of raiders. In two weeks, the last of them was on its way toward the passes, harried by vengeful Lords and even by some peasants. Apparently Blade wasn't the only Lord along the Crimson River who had looked the other way while the unlordly armed themselves.

The victory was expensive; it did not touch the heart of

King Fedron's main army, and it came too late for many people. Among these was Romiss the Breeder. A band of raiders captured him while he was visiting a friend in the village near his castle. They took him to the castle and threatened to torture him to death if the men inside did not open the gates.

"Don't give these swine a thing!" Romiss shouted, before he was silenced.

Romiss's men were accustomed to obeying his orders and did not open the gates. Instead they watched as the Breeder was blinded, then castrated, then burned with hot irons. After that, Alsin rode up and scattered the raiders, in time to save the castle, but too late to do anything for Romiss except give him a quick death.

"No man in all the Duchies died a more lordly death," said Alsin when Blade rode back to Castle Ranit and heard the news. "The men of the castle have asked for arms, in order to defend it if there is another attack."

"There will be," said Blade. "And this time from Fedron's whole army."

"I know." Alsin seemed unwilling to look at Blade. "So I have given them arms, to use within the castle itself. No sane Lord can say I should leave them helpless, to die like Romiss!"

"No." So Romiss was dead, and all the secrets of the origins of the Feathered Ones were gone with him. But right now this seemed like a small detail to Blade, who excused himself and went up to see Miera.

She was barely conscious, not even enough to recognize him, and after a few minutes, she slipped back into sleep. Blade sat by the bed until Sarylla came and led him away for a drink. She looked almost as bad as her patient by now—gaunt, red-eyed, her glossy black hair faded and hanging in strings.

Now bad news and good news followed each other in swift succession. First they heard that Chenosh had signed an alliance with King Handryg of the West Kingdom. Next they heard that King Fedron was preparing to invade with his main army. Then they heard that Chenosh was returning, bringing some of Handryg's Lords with him, to wait until King Handryg himself arrived with the rest of his army and supply wagons. Finally, they heard on the same day that King Fedron's army had crossed the border and that Miera was showing signs of pneumonia. A few moments later, the girl was fighting for her life, while the King's army was marching straight on the Duchy of Nainan.

After they learned of Fedron's proximity, everyone was too busy preparing Castle Ranit to stand a siege and serve as a base for the army of the Duchies to sympathize with Blade. But he did not miss the sympathy. In his present mood, he was glad to be left alone.

It was going to be a cloudy day, so they wouldn't have to fight in a blazing sun. Blade was glad of that. He didn't find much else to be glad about.

As he was riding down the line of the Duchies' army to his place on the left wing, a thought struck him. Here he was in a scene that came straight out of the pages of a medieval romance. He was a valiant knight going into battle, prepared to do mighty deeds of valor almost under the walls of the castle where his fair lady waited.

Very pretty. Except that he didn't feel valiant; he felt tired and angry. Any deeds he did today would serve mostly to save his own life and those of the men around him from a ruthless enemy. And his fair lady was a shrunken, doll-like figure in a great bed, unconscious, gasping for each breath, and unlikely to live through the day.

He swung his long-handled mace through the air until it hummed. He was in a thoroughly bloodthirsty mood. With half his mind he remembered that this might make him careless. With the other half he hoped it would make him a better fighter.

He reined in on the extreme left flank of the army. There were five thousand Lords, drawn up on horseback and on foot, with two thousand Helpers guarding the horses and baggage. It was the largest army ever raised along the Crimson River and included fighters from every Duchy except Faissa. There were too few trustworthy men from the late Duke Klaman's army still in shape to fight.

They faced an opponent who outnumbered them almost two to one. King Fedron had six thousand Lords on the field, five thousand mounted infantrymen with pikes, and a thousand odds and ends to guard his baggage. Individually, his men weren't as tough as the Lords of the Crimson River, but they had discipline to add to their edge in numbers.

If only King Handryg's army had come! But there was no sign that King Handryg or his army even existed, except for the two hundred Lords he'd sent on ahead. Blade could see their banners near Chenosh's. King Handryg was bringing a ponderous train of wagons loaded with supplies, and they were slowing his march to a crawl. The supplies made sense, if Handryg expected a long war. But if only he had come fast enough to be here today and guarantee victory, he wouldn't have to worry about a long war!

Was Handryg planning to let the two armies tear each other to pieces and then rule the whole Dimension himself? His reputation made this seem unlikely, but not impossible.

Trumpets and drums sounded, and a column of pikemen thrust itself out from the Eastern lines. They marched with an impressively steady tread, chanting as they came. Blade called one of the Helpers over, then scratched Cheeky's back and handed him down to the young man. A battle on this scale was no place for a feather-monkey, even Cheeky, who was as tough as a Feathered One could be. The creature was the one friend Blade had in this Dimension that he could try to keep safe from today's battle.

Cheeky's *yeeeep* of protest was lost in the din as the pikemen reached the Duchies' lines. They struck close to Duke Padro's banner, and for a moment Blade saw it wavering. Then it steadied, and he saw the towering figures of Padro's bodyguards taking their place around the banner bearer. Even at this distance, they loomed over the men around them.

Blade quickly saw that their strength wasn't going to be sufficient. The pikemen were pressing forward, driving a steel-tipped wedge into Padro's ranks. From among the pikes, swordsmen darted forward, stabbing at faces or chinks in armor with their short thrusting weapons. The swordsmen wore little armor, but against Lords who didn't have room to use their weapons freely they didn't need much.

168

When Blade saw that the Helper who was carrying Cheeky was out of the way, he signaled to his trumpeter. The trumpet's call gathered up Blade's Guardsmen and urged them forward after him at a trot. They curled around Padro's rear and plunged into the dust cloud rising from the front lines. The sun wasn't out, but there'd been no rain for many days. The ground was powder dry.

Once inside the dust cloud, it was every man for himself. Blade controlled his horse with his knees as he fended off pike thrusts with his shield, and splintered pike shafts and crushed skulls with his mace. A swordsman darted forward, stabbing at the belly of Blade's horse, but it was well trained. It snapped its teeth in the swordsman's face, and he jumped back. Before he could close again, one of Padro's courtiers hacked off his sword arm with a battle-ax, and Blade's mace came down on his head. He fell into the dust, which was now turning into a red mud, where dying men wallowed and screamed under the trampling of men and horses.

After a while, the trumpets and drums sounded again, the swordsmen ran back under the protection of the pikes, and the pikemen themselves withdrew. Duke Padro's banner was still standing, but the Duke himself was being carried away by the only four of his bodyguards who remained on their feet. His olive complexion was now ashen and gray from the loss of blood that followed half a dozen wounds. However he had lived, Blade hoped it would be remembered that Padro of Gualdar died like a warrior and a man.

So the battle went all morning. The Eastern pikemen would advance, the swordsmen would leap into battle, and men would die thick and fast. But the pikemen never broke through the Duchies' lines. Though they always caused many casualties, they withdrew before they suffered nearly as many themselves. They were slowly but surely whittling down the Duchies' strength, and meanwhile the Eastern cavalry was still almost intact. When the two mounted forces did meet, each Lord of the Crimson River was worth two of his opponents. They didn't meet often.

Slowly the battle took the shape of a U, with the sides

formed by the Eastern cavalry and the bottom formed by their infantry. The Duchies' army was inside the U, with only the top as a way out. Blade suspected that King Fedron could close that escape route any time he wanted to if he threw in the last of his cavalry. That he was still keeping it out of the fight suggested that he too was wondering where King Handryg might be.

More attacks, more dead, and now men on both sides were falling from thirst, exhaustion, and the inhalation of too much dust. Blade scraped crusted human remains off his mace with his dagger, drank some water, and led his Guardsmen back into the fight. In places he felt as if he were riding through a London fog, except that he'd never heard so many screams of men and horses and so much clashing steel on the streets of London. He'd never been so hot or thirsty in London, either.

What must have been at least the twentieth attack faded away. Blade heard trumpets with a new note in them and, moments later, wild cheering. He looked to the rear and saw two massive columns of horsemen approaching. The banners of the West Kingdom floated from jeweled staffs, which sparkled even through the dust.

King Handryg was coming, at last. Now the battle could not be lost, although it might take a good deal more fighting to win it. Blade wished he could feel better, but he was too thirsty and too aware of how many things could still go wrong. He was also a little too cynical about the ability of the Lords of the Crimson River to win a victory if there was no "honor" in it.

The horsemen divided, passing to the right and left of the embattled armies. To the right went six or seven thousand Lords. To the left went more than two thousand men mounted on small horses and carrying pikes or spears, with leather-wrapped bundles on their backs. More mounted infantry, Blade guessed. He wondered why they were riding so far out to the left. They'd be out of reach of any help if Fedron decided to attack them.

Then it was as if someone waved a magic wand over the two thousand. Most of them leaped from their saddles, then thrust their spears into the ground. As the horse holders moved off, the men on the ground planted an impenetrable hedge of jutting spears in front of them. Then they unslung the bundles from their backs and unwrapped them. Now, in the hands of each one of fifteen hundred men gleamed a crossbow.

A terrible silence descended on the battlefield, as everyone seemed to hold his breath. Blade knew what had to be coming next; he wondered how many others did.

It came. Fifteen hundred archers cocked their bows, dropped bolts into place, lifted them, and shot. Bolts poured down like hail, onto the mounted Lords of the East Kingdom.

Each of the archers must have picked a target, and most of them were good shots. A thousand bolts must have found targets in men or horses and all the horses and most of the men seemed to be screaming at once. Gone was the silence, and what replaced it sounded like the end of the world. In the uproar Blade also heard curses and cries of horror from the Duchies' ranks. The sight of men, even enemies, dying in such an unlordly fashion was more than they could bear in silence.

Certainly this was nearly the end of the battle. As the archers shot again, the Lords of the West on the other flank charged. It was a wild, disorderly charge, and for a while it only kicked up dust. Before the dust grew too thick, though, Blade saw Lords of the East begin to turn their horses. They'd already lost their chances of an easy victory. Now they faced a good chance of a messy, unlordly death. Whatever loyalty they owed their King wasn't enough to make them hold still for that.

At the bottom of the U, Fedron's banner still rose behind his pikemen. He was trying to rally them. Blade was willing to leave that part of the fight to stronger men on fresher horses. He led his Guardsmen back toward the baggage and the water.

By now the shock of seeing Lords struck down by archers was wearing off. Everyone who still had a voice seemed to be expressing an opinion. Most of the opinions were what Blade expected.

"Unlordly!"

"Lawless!"

"An abomination!"

"The Fathers will not bless a victory won this way!"

"We fought properly, at least."

"Yes, but we can't allow ourselves to gain by the victory, or—"

And then an exchange which froze Blade in his saddle:

"At least King Fedron fought a lordly battle."

"Yes. If we are to have a King, let it be Fedron. I'll swear no oath to Handryg."

"My steel on that!"

"Yes, and my steel *for* anyone who says a word for Handryg. That—"

Blade's first impulse was to splatter the brains of those two idiots with his mace. Then he realized that they probably had no brains, only firm prejudices, probably shared by many of their fellow Lords. Prejudices enough to create two factions in the Duchies: those who wanted to swear allegiance to King Handryg and those who preferred King Fedron. Only a miracle would keep the two factions from coming to blows. Then there would be war all over again along the Crimson River, a civil war likely to go on until the land was a barren waste. All the deaths Blade had seen since he reached this Dimension would be wasted, and thousands more would die.

Such a thought would have paralyzed most men. It made Blade think and move faster than usual, even after a long day of battle. *If King Fedron is dead, nobody is going to be swearing anything to him.* Then he looked down the battlefield to where the East Kingdom's banner still waved, and dug in his spurs.

As his horse gathered speed, Blade passed close to the Helper who held Cheeky. With an eager cry the Feathered One hurled himself through the air, landing on the head of Blade's mount. The horse shied and Blade reached down, meaning to pluck Cheeky loose and toss him back to safety. But Cheeky refused to budge, clinging to the horse's ears until the animal started to rear.

All right, thought Blade. *You, too, have more courage than sense.*

The legends of later years said that the ranks of the enemy gave way before Lord Blade Duke-Slayer as if by magic. Some stories said that the look in his eyes turned men to stone, or at least made them drop their weapons. He certainly looked dangerous enough, but the fact was that the East Kingdom's pikemen were already breaking ranks when he rode up. He had to be careful not to step on bodies or press too closely against men already turning to run, but he wasn't in much danger from the men on foot.

The mounted Lords around Fedron might well have been another matter, but as Blade approached them, Alsin ordered a general attack. He'd seen Blade ride into the ranks of the enemy. Even if Blade was determined to die, honor required the men of Nainan to try to save him. And then again, if *he*, Alsin, didn't lead the attack, Chenosh would, and if Chenosh died, Alsin didn't even want to think about what might happen.

So he attacked, and King Fedron sent his bodyguards forward to help the pikemen. The Eastern king was almost alone when Blade rode up to him. He was not turned to stone, though, and he didn't drop his sword. He was a warrior to the last, and he nearly killed his opponent.

The two men circled each other on horseback, mace and sword crashing against shields. On the fourth stroke the sword split Blade's battered shield and numbed his left arm. Fedron drove his horse in close and his own mount snapped at Blade's thigh. Blade felt the teeth dent his flesh through the mail.

Then Cheeky leaped to his master's defense, hurling himself onto the head of Fedron's mount. He covered the horse's eyes, and it reared in panic. Fedron was off-balance, and a sword stroke intended to split his enemy's head only cut the air. Blade swung his mace and caught the King in the chest, as his horse reared again and threw him backward. The combined force of horse and mace was too much. Fedron went backward out of the saddle with a scream. Before he could struggle to his feet, his bodyguards broke under Alsin's charge. So King Fedron died—under the hooves of his own fleeing bodyguards.

Blade didn't wait to help identify the battered royal corpse. With Cheeky on his shoulder, he rode back through the Duchies' army, ignoring the cheers. He rode straight to

173

Castle Ranit, then went up to the room in the keep where his wife lay.

He did not leave it or speak to anyone there until Miera died just before sunset.

Chapter 24

About half the mounted Lords with King Fedron died, most of them under the archery. The rest were already on their way off the field when they heard of their King's death. This news made them move even faster. King Handryg's army made no attempt to pursue, and the Lords of the Crimson River were too exhausted to even try.

So the battle died down well before sunset. Alsin finished the day by making sure the two armies camped well apart. The Lords of the Duchies resented Handryg's late arrival as well as his unlordly tactics. At the same time, the Eastern army seemed ready to carry off every unattached woman and stray animal in Nainan.

"Blade will be amused to hear of your trying to protect women and chickens," said Chenosh, as they rode toward the castle.

"I doubt Blade will find anything amusing for some time," said Alsin heavily.

Chenosh flushed under his coating of dust. "I'm sorry. You are quite right. He—"

"Never mind. If he *was* amused, he would be right. But—what else could I do?" He asked the question of the empty air and got no answer. They rode on in silence for a while.

Then Chenosh spoke up again. "Alsin, Fedron is dead, and I do not see how we can get our Lords to trust Handryg. I am not sure I trust him myself, and it is not just because of the archers."

"No. He could have come sooner, if his heart was in it. We had food and wine enough in Nainan for all his men and horses. Those wagons of his were an excuse."

"Or perhaps he didn't want to take any food from us. That way he would be freer to turn against us anytime he chose."

Alsin nodded. He and Chenosh saw clearly that King Handryg was not now, and never could be, an acceptable ruler for the Duchies. On the other hand, with the East Kingdom in chaos, he might not be interested in the Duchies anymore. He might have his eyes on a bigger prize and his hand outstretched to grab it. This prospect could make it easier to do what Alsin knew must be done, but only if he acted quickly. And he could only act quickly if Chenosh agreed at once—tonight, if possible.

Alsin saw the other riders had dropped back a little and pulled his horse up close to Chenosh. "Your Grace," he said formally.

"Yes, Marshal?"

"You will doubtless be wanting to hold a ducal audience, as soon as possible. But I would like a talk with you alone first."

"You will have my ear, Alsin. It is the least you deserve, after all you have done. As long as you mean nothing against Lord Blade."

"Nothing at all, Your Grace."

Blade stepped away from the bed as the women finished laying Miera out. With her shorn head concealed by a cap and the pain gone from her face, she looked more like the woman he'd known than she had since her wounding.

He was no longer feeling sorry for himself. Self-pity was basically a futile emotion, and one he drove out as fast as he could. There were also a great many more people in the Duchies worse off than he was, thanks to this war. It was time to do something for them.

He'd start with Sarylla. She was standing at the head of the bed, making sure that her assistants did everything right. She was now as determined to see Miera properly

175

buried as she had been to save her. But she'd used up the last of her own strength nursing the girl. If she didn't rest it would soon be a question of *her* funeral. She'd also need some money, and since Blade would be getting a handsome share of the day's loot . . .

A knock sounded on the door to the stair, then a voice said, "Lord Blade. It is Duke Chenosh. May I come in?"

The women stepped hastily aside as the young Duke entered, followed by Alsin and Lord Gennar. Chenosh stood by the bed for a moment, his lips moving in a short prayer to the Fathers. Then he turned to Blade. His face was a mask which the older man didn't even try to read.

"Lord Blade, Marshal Alsin and I have decided that the Duchies must . follow a new path. Handryg cannot be trusted, and Fedron is dead. So we cannot offer our allegiance to either Kingdom. We must found a Kingdom of our own." The mask broke, and Blade saw in Chenosh the look of a man who must walk a tightrope over a bottomless canyon in order to save his life.

"We must found a Kingdom of our own," he repeated. "So I am going to proclaim myself King. King of the Realm of the Crimson River. And my first act as King will be—"

"To proclaim Marshal Alsin as the new Duke of Nainan," said Blade, interrupting without thinking.

Chenosh laughed at the surprise on Alsin's face. "Are you *sure* he doesn't read men's minds?" he said. Then he nodded.

Blade would have knelt to both men, but his knees were too stiff. "Your Grace," he said to the Marshal. "If you are going to be giving out rewards and punishments in Nainan, I would like to ask a favor of you. As your first act, the woman Sarylla should—"

"No!" said Gennar suddenly. The others stared at him as he crossed the room and put his arms around Sarylla. "The *Lady* Sarylla may be rewarded if it is Marshal—I mean, Duke—Alsin's pleasure to do so. But first of all, I am going to take her as my lawful, lordly wife. If she will have me," he added. He swallowed, and Blade saw that the warrior Lord was frightened half out of his wits at the idea of Sarylla refusing him.

Fortunately for everybody, she managed to gasp out the word "yes" before she fainted into Gennar's arms. He and the women took her out to another chamber, leaving Blade, Alsin, and Chenosh staring at each other.

Alsin was the first to get his voice back. "Well, if I can be a Duke, then surely Sarylla can be a lady. She is probably better fitted for her task than I am for mine. Nonetheless, I do have that task. And the first proclamation *I* will make is that Lord Blade is Marshal of Nainan."

There was clearly no safe or easy way to refuse, so Blade didn't. In fact, he felt like cheering. Alsin's appointing him Marshal meant his work in arming the peasants was accepted, and that the new Duke's mind was open to the idea of further changes. "I will accept," he said. "But on the condition that Lord Gennar be made my second in command, and Lord Ebass be given command of the Duke's Guardsmen."

"Done," said Alsin, and Blade gave a mental sigh of relief. Both Gennar and Ebass deserved rewards, and now they had them. Also, Gennar was another man who could cope with all the changes that were happening to warfare along the Crimson River.

There was no need to talk of details now, and certainly not here, with Miera's sightless eyes on them. "Although I feel more easy in my mind about my grandfather's death and Miera's now," said Chenosh, "I feel—well, I feel that his work will go on, and his death will not be a waste."

When the two visitors went downstairs, Blade turned the other way and climbed onto the roof of the keep. Cheeky rode on his shoulder. The sky was clearing now, and the wind was brisk enough to feel cool on his skin. It felt even better in his lungs after the thick air of the death room.

Overhead, the stars were coming out. Blade leaned against the stone battlements, then hastily stepped back as he felt a stone shift under his weight. A fine end to this trip and his life it would be, falling through the battlements and splattering on the ground a hundred and fifty feet below!

He took a deep breath and opened his mind to Cheeky. He hadn't spoken with the Feathered One for days, and he wanted to see how the battle looked through his eyes.

"Yeeeeeppp!"

Blade heard surprise and even pain in the Feathered One's call. Then he felt a prickling all over his skin and a throbbing in his head, just below the threshold of pain but impossible to ignore. For a moment he understood Cheeky's surprise and even shared it. Then the throbbing grew more intense, and although it still wasn't painful, he recognized it.

The computer was calling to him, ready to bring him back to Home Dimension. Because Cheeky was linked to his mind, the computer was calling to him, too. In fact, he'd picked up the call before Blade did, but didn't know what it meant.

It was easier for Blade to control his thoughts with this new form of the computer's call. He told Cheeky to keep calm, and at the same time scratched his back in the familiar manner.

For a moment the throbbing flared to pain. Blade braced himself against a firm section of stone. He heard Cheeky *yeeeep* again, the world swam in front of his eyes . . .

. . . and he was standing in the transfer booth, with Cheeky still on his shoulder.

The Feathered One's next *yeeeep* was rather subdued.

Chapter 25

". . . refuse to use the word 'apologize' under the circumstances."

"Richard, there's no point in not calling a spade a spade. I realize you're reluctant to save Lord Leighton's pride after what he said to you—"

"You're bloody right I'm reluctant!"

"—but do you see anything else to do? Richard, if you're going to be stubborn about this, I'm going to question the soundness of your judgment."

"Is that a threat?"

"It is not," said J in the chilliest voice Blade could recall hearing him use in years. "It's simply a statement of fact."

It was on the tip of his tongue to ask J what right he had to try making up the quarrel between Blade and Lord Leighton, considering how he'd lost his temper with the scientist not too long ago, but refrained. If he said it, there'd simply be a quarrel with J added to the one with Lord Leighton.

"I'll talk to you tomorrow," he said briskly to J, and hung up. It was the first time he'd hung up on J. He felt that he was showing rather a lot of self-restraint in not slamming the receiver down.

He went over to the sideboard and poured himself a large whiskey. It was only his second of the evening. He didn't plan to get drunk—not tonight. He wasn't that angry yet.

"*Yeeeep?*"

"All right, Cheeky. You can have something, too."

Blade opened another can of preserved fruit and added some salted nuts, then poured the mixture into a bowl and set it on the sideboard. Cheeky jumped up and began munching happily, his tail waving back and forth.

Good thing nobody can see how happy he is, thought Blade. *They'd suspect my story*. Blade had claimed that because of their telepathic link, he and Cheeky had developed a strong bond, and the feather-monkey would refuse to eat if Blade was not present. Thus Cheeky would have to stay with him until he adjusted to Home Dimension. The Project scientists were too afraid of losing the creature not to let Blade have his way. So the Feathered One came home with his master. There he would stay, if not until hell froze over, at least for a month or two.

If the scientists suspected that he had lied to keep Cheeky away from them, however, they would have fits. They would also join forces with Lord Leighton, and then all the scientific staff of Project Dimension X would be on bad terms with Richard Blade. He knew that before this

179

happened, he'd have to back down. As little as he liked the idea of eating crow, he knew he'd do it if the alternative was wrecking the Project.

Indeed, it appeared that the earlier squabble between Leighton and J over the spymaster's intelligence work was minor in comparison with the state of affairs in the Project now. As soon as Blade had returned from Dimension X, everybody began yelling at everybody else. Leighton was furious because Blade had brought back only a monkey and nothing else, even failing to return with the shorts and sandals. Blade could hardly control his voice as he explained that these "clothes" didn't even make good underwear, and that from the looks he got when he first appeared in Dimension X, he'd have been better off stark naked, the way he usually was when he arrived. At least the commando knife had proved useful, and he had returned with *that*, though he would have preferred a weapon more like those used in the other Dimension. Then Leighton and J both began questioning Blade's powers of judgment for not finding out about the metal reflector and the mysterious Fathers, and Blade lost all patience as he angrily explained that his attachments to people in other Dimensions sometimes took priority over learning the mysteries of their lands. By the time the meeting ended, no one was talking to anyone else, and it seemed that for all anyone cared the Project could collapse.

Blade was going to have to do something, but he wasn't going to do it soon, no matter what J said! If Lord Leighton was going to say things like "Richard's more loyal to the girls he picks up in Dimension X than he is to the Project," he bloody well ought to stew in his own juice for a few days! No doubt Leighton and J had reason to be angry about Blade's failure to learn anything about the origins of the Feathered Ones or the reflector. But most of the failure wasn't his fault, and there was absolutely no call to insult Miera's memory. None at all.

Blade discovered that his whiskey was gone and considered pouring a third. He hadn't yet made up his mind when there was a knock on the door.

It was one of the Special Branch men assigned to the Project, with a small attaché case chained to his wrist.

"Mr. Blade? A letter for you, from Lord Leighton. You'll have to sign for it."

Blade got out a pen. It seemed unlikely that Leighton had reached the point of sending him letter bombs. He signed for the letter but waited until the door was closed and locked before opening it.

It was a good thing he did. When he'd read the letter and looked at the other item in the envelope, he poured himself a third whiskey. Then he sat down and read the letter again. If he read it often enough, he might really believe it.

Dear Richard,

I apologize for everything I said in connection with what you did or left undone in the Dimension of the Crimson River. Absolutely, and without reservation, I apologize. It was not your fault that you could not learn more about the origins of the Feathered Ones. Even if it was, I had no right to insult the memory of Miera, for whom you obviously cared very much.

I have never married, never contemplated doing so, and never really missed it. My work has always given me as much order in my life as I needed. I am not sure that you are the same type of man.

I'd also like to mention that my hopes for the Project have grown by leaps and bounds, now that we've all had a chance to calm down. I won't even try to keep secret from J and his spies the fact that our new field-generator booth is a total success, and that I have great plans for eventually sending you and your feather-monkey friend to Dimension X. I also have some ideas for a new weapon we can send with you, and I've come up with an outfit I think you'll really like.

Meanwhile, I understand you have been thinking of buying a country house. I don't know how far your plans have gone, but it would certainly be a step in the right direction if you did so. I therefore enclose this contribution to your house fund.

Yours sincerely,
Leighton

"This contribution" was a check on Lloyd's Bank for twenty-five thousand pounds.

Blade read the letter a third time, poured himself a

fourth whiskey, then carefully put the check in his pocket. His fellow human beings were the kind of mysteries that made Dimension X look simple and predictable. This wasn't a new discovery, but he'd seldom had the fact shoved in his face this way!

He sipped at his whiskey and scratched Cheeky all over from his head to the base of his tail. So now he would have a companion after all, traveling with him to Dimension X. But Blade put such thoughts out of his mind so that he could concentrate on the present. He took out the check and looked at it again. Twenty-five thousand pounds— *more* than enough to buy and rebuild that house in Hampshire. He'd telephone the real-estate people in the morning.

Then, with any luck, he could have a month to himself, during which he wouldn't even need to remember that there *was* such a place as Dimension X.